BENEATH
SOUTHERN SKIES

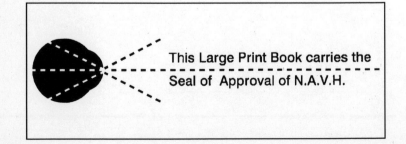

This Large Print Book carries the
Seal of Approval of N.A.V.H.

BENEATH SOUTHERN SKIES

TERRA LITTLE

THORNDIKE PRESS

A part of Gale, Cengage Learning

GALE
CENGAGE Learning·

Farmington Hills, Mich • San Francisco • New York • Waterville, Maine
Meriden, Conn • Mason, Ohio • Chicago

GALE
CENGAGE Learning®

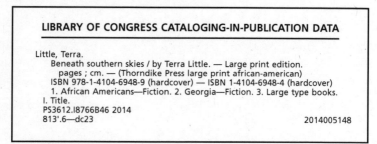

LIBRARY OF CONGRESS CATALOGING-IN-PUBLICATION DATA

Little, Terra.
  Beneath southern skies / by Terra Little. — Large print edition.
    pages ; cm. — (Thorndike Press large print african-american)
  ISBN 978-1-4104-6948-9 (hardcover) — ISBN 1-4104-6948-4 (hardcover)
  1. African Americans—Fiction. 2. Georgia—Fiction. 3. Large type books.
  I. Title.
  PS3612.I8766B46 2014
  813'.6—dc23   2014005148

Published in 2014 by arrangement with Harlequin Books S.A.

Printed in Mexico
1 2 3 4 5 6 7 18 17 16 15 14

This one is for my family, which will soon include a new addition — my very first grandchild.

Many thanks to all of the readers who continue to support me and my work. I hope this one does you proud.

PROLOGUE

The longer Tressie Valentine held the stack of official-looking papers and read, the more the hand holding them trembled. They were the answer to all her prayers, or at least they could be if what she was reading was really true.

Suddenly finding herself unemployed and penniless was a predicament that Tressie had never envisioned for herself, and she'd been on the verge of pulling her hair out by the roots ever since that predicament had become her reality.

But now, if there was a God in heaven and she hadn't managed to completely alienate Him, it looked as though the streak of bad luck that she'd been riding hard and fast for the past two months was about to take a sharp turn for the better. God knew she needed some good luck right about now.

In a matter of weeks, what little savings she'd managed to accumulate over the past five years had quickly dwindled down to little more than enough to keep a roof over her head for the next couple of months. She didn't even want to think about all the other unpaid bills that were steadily pouring in. When had she applied for so many credit cards? Amassed so many lines of private store credit? Gotten so out of control with her spending? Of course, it hadn't seemed as if her spending was out of control while she was safely ensconced in the luxury of a six-figure salary and living the high life. But the blinders were off, and she knew that she was in serious trouble.

This summons, or whatever it was, that had landed in her mailbox this morning could be just what she needed to help her get her life back on track.

Snuggled deep in the luxurious recesses of a thick cashmere robe, papers in hand, Tressie plopped down on the leather sofa in the great room of her twentieth-floor loft apartment and reached for the cordless phone on a nearby end table. Her toes curled into the thick pile of the specially ordered Oriental rug underneath her bare feet as she punched in the telephone number listed at the top of the document. Praying that the estimated quote on the page in front of her wasn't a typo, she listened to the phone ring on the other end and then smiled when a woman's cheerful voice finally greeted her. Just this morning she had been seriously considering pitching a tent out on the sidewalk, clearing out her designer label–filled walk-in closet and hosting a yard sale to stave off the wolves at her door. But now . . . now things were looking up and not a moment too soon.

"Could I please speak with Norman Harper?" Tressie asked after the woman had finished rattling off the string of names listed on the company's letterhead. "Please tell him that Tressie Valentine is calling."

"Just a moment while I transfer you," the woman said. Seconds later, Tressie was listening to classical music and humming along as her thoughts wandered.

Soon enough, Saul Worthington and the rest of the schmucks at the *New York Inquisitor* would realize that they had made a big mistake by cutting her loose. By now, Tressie Valentine, better known as Vanessa Valentino to her loyal and discriminating readers, was a household name. Knowing that, Saul, as the *Inquisitor*'s editor-in-chief, hadn't even bothered to print a formal announcement that she had severed ties with the paper. Instead, he had chosen to simply omit her weekly column and replace it with a lackluster new weekly feature on education reform. It was a show, she knew, of blatant disrespect and one that she would never forget. And it was the worst mistake he could've ever made. No, scratch that — it was the second-worst mistake he could've ever made.

Firing her had definitely been the worst.

The whole scene had been unbelievable, like something out of badly scripted sitcom rerun. Even now as she thought back on it, she felt the humiliation and ridiculousness of it all over again, as if it were happening right now. It was true that hindsight was your best sight, but even in hindsight she couldn't quite figure out where she'd gone wrong. One minute she'd had the upper hand and the next, everything had spiraled out of her control. One minute she was gainfully employed and the next she was spending her days catching up on all the soap operas that she'd missed over the years and worrying about what her future held. How, she wondered for the millionth time, had she lost the upper hand?

"Fired? I'm fired?" Tressie had been in a state of shock, looking around the handsomely appointed executive office of the *New York Inquisitor* as if she'd never seen it before, except, of course, she had, many times. It'd only been a month ago that everyone had been crowded into the office, pouring champagne and toasting her Delilah Award nomination. Ultimately, she hadn't actually won the coveted journalism award, but just the fact that she'd been counted among the handful of female journalists who were worthy of recognition had been a feather in Saul's cap. Now she was fired?

"Saul?" Tressie had prompted when Saul had only stared at her. Uncharacteristically silent, his forehead was crinkled into a million deep-set worry lines, and his bright red power tie was crooked, as if he had been yanking on it nonstop. Under her steady gaze, his face reddened guiltily. "Please tell me I heard you incorrectly, because I think you just said that I was fired. But that can't possibly be right. I'm the best damn columnist you have around here and if it weren't for me —"

"Tressie . . ." Saul sighed, his eyes looking everywhere but at her. "I received a call from Gary Price's people this afternoon."

Finally, something that made sense. All this talk about firing her was just his way of decompressing after what had to have been a nerve-racking phone conversation. He was upset, probably a little out of sorts, too, but that was to be expected. Stories like the one she'd written tended to shake up the usual order of things, which as far as she was concerned was exactly as it should be. Saul didn't always agree with her investigative methods, but they had always managed to see eye to eye where the bottom line was concerned. Her story, just like all the others before it, had dollar signs stamped all over it, and frantic phone calls from guilty parties was the confirmation that she'd hit the jackpot, yet again.

She perked up, scooting to the edge of her chair and slapping her hands down on her side of Saul's desk. "Good. What did they have to say for their golden boy?"

His ocean-blue eyes narrowed until they were slits in his face. "They're pissed."

"Well, they should be," Tressie decided, flopping back in her chair and rearranging her Calvin Klein suit jacket around her. "He's been out of control for a while now. They should've known that I'd get around to calling him out sooner or later. It had to be done, Saul, and I hope you told them that." A derisive laugh slipped past her lips before she could stop it. "*His people.* Please. Who has people anymore? No one is beyond my reach, people or no people."

"I warned you about going after Gary

Price, and if you had listened —"

"If I had listened, the world wouldn't know that Gary Price tried to bribe his way into a vacant senatorial seat while he was carrying on an affair with the current governor's wife, and right after he managed to weasel his way out of being charged with embezzling charitable funds from the state." She threw up her hands and let them fall back to her lap wearily. "Who does that?"

Saul snatched off his glasses, dropped them on his desk and scrubbed at his eyelids with stiff fingers. He looked so distraught that she almost felt sorry for him. It was on the tip of her tongue to offer a halfhearted apology for her part in his misery, but the next words out of his mouth dashed any warm and fuzzy feelings that might've been brewing inside her.

"According to Gary Price's attorney, he doesn't. They're suing the paper, Tressie, which brings me back to the reason I asked to meet with you."

"So you could fire me for being a damn good columnist? Come on, Saul, that makes about as much sense as you bowing to non-existent pressure from Gary Price's mysterious people. Since when do you care about ruffling a few feathers? It's the nature of the business. You used to know that."

"We can't afford a lawsuit right now," Saul bit out in a shrill tone that Tressie had never heard before. A few more wrinkles appeared in his forehead and an accusing finger pointed in her direction. "*You* should know that. I don't need to remind you about who was partly to blame for the paper having to file bankruptcy last year, do I?"

Already knowing where the conversation was going and not wanting to touch the subject with a ten-foot pole, she waved a dismissive hand to cut him off. "So promise him a retraction in tomorrow's paper or a front-page apology. Just don't make me write it, because I won't. He won't know the difference anyway, and we've done it plenty of times before."

Confident that she had pushed all the right buttons, sufficiently made her point and put the conversation back on track, Tressie straightened her tailored black skirt around her thighs and crossed her legs. Her right foot swung back and forth in the air purposefully while her thoughts focused in on her latest target. Gary Price was quickly becoming a heavy hitter in the local political arena, that much was true, but he was no different from the hundreds, maybe even thousands, of other schmucks that she'd written about over the years. It'd taken her a decade to accomplish it, but by now everyone who was anyone knew who she was and what she did, even though she did it pretty much anonymously. She was *the* Vanessa Valentino, the gossip columnist who wasn't afraid to go where even the infamous Rona Barrett had never gone, and she had pissed off much more important people than the likes of Gary Price — a washed-up politician who, for a laughably brief period, had tried his hand at acting and failed dismally.

Why was Saul so bent out of shape over this story? There was always an instant uproar when the Saturday edition of the *Inquisitor* hit the newsstands and her weekly column made its rounds, but it always died down in anticipation of her next column. It was a cycle, and Saul had never bothered to interfere with it before. So, why now?

Sure, he'd threatened to suspend her once or twice over the years, and she vaguely recalled narrowly avoiding being demoted not so long ago — but fired? It was inconceivable. He needed her too much. If ever there was a cash cow, she was it.

"A retraction is the least of my worries right now, Tressie." Saul gestured to a stack of legal-looking papers on his desktop and blew out a strong breath. "We were served with notice of the lawsuit this morning, which means that we don't have very much time to clean up this mess. Price is suing the *Inquisitor* for upward of ten million dollars, and we simply don't have the firepower to strike back. To put it bluntly, we're broke." Her mouth dropped open as Saul went on. "The legal department is on it, but they've suggested that I make a few preemptive moves to pacify Price and his attorneys in the meantime."

"Such as?"

His tone, when he spoke, was final. "Such as suspending you indefinitely."

"You can't do that. You need me," Tressie said before she could think better of it.

"You're impulsive," he snapped. "You act without thinking. You go right for the throat, consequences be damned, and you never seem to think about how your actions affect everyone else."

"But that's what makes me a good columnist, Saul," Tressie sputtered helplessly. She sensed that she was losing ground, and the feeling was as unsettling as the determined set of Saul's mouth. "Before I became Vanessa Valentino, the *Inquisitor* was the laughingstock of New York. You were printing stories about snakes with two heads, secret underground cities in third-world countries, and sending out interns to track Bigfoot through Central Park. No respectable newspaper, here or anywhere else, would even take your calls. I'm the reason you have that impressive trophy case over there." She threw out a hand and pointed at the case in question. It was a glass-and-chrome monstrosity that took up most of the wall to the right of his equally monstrous desk, and, currently, it was nearly overflowing with awards and plaques that Vanessa Valentino had received over the years. "I'm the reason there's even anything in it. My impulsiveness put those awards there. My go-for-the-throat philosophy put this paper on the map, and you know it. You fire me and you'll lose it all."

"What I need," Saul cut in tersely, "is a columnist who isn't single-handedly the biggest threat to the very existence of this newspaper, Tressie. In the last five years alone you've managed to cost us hundreds of thousands of dollars in legal fees, bribes, payoffs and hush money." He blew out a long, strong breath and gritted his teeth. "Hell, the cost of keeping your true identity secret is expensive enough as it is. The nonstop threat of being sued penniless has had me wondering for a while now if you're more trouble than you're worth and —" he ruffled the papers in front of him so roughly that they spread out like a fan across the desktop "— now I guess I don't have to wonder anymore. I can't let you cause the paper any more problems, Tressie. The lawsuits and bad publicity stop right here. Right now. Enough is enough."

It was impossible not to follow what he was saying. She understood him clearly and, as hurtful as his words were, she thought that he needed to understand something, too. "My readers are loyal. They'll go where I go."

That, Tressie decided on a long sigh, was where she'd gone wrong. She'd never actually seen the top of a man's head blow off, but Saul had come very close to making that impossible feat a reality. He was already tall and stocky, but when he'd shot up out of his chair and towered over his desk, she could've sworn that rage had caused him to grow another six inches in height and expand at least another foot in width. The bravado that she'd been holding on to by a thread had quickly vanished, along with any hope that she'd had of holding on to her job. Saul's parting shot — "I'll call you if anything changes" — had rung in her ears as she was escorted out of the building like some common criminal.

Ten years, she couldn't help thinking with every step she'd taken out the doors. Ten years of her life had gone up in smoke just like that. She'd scratched and scraped, begged and pleaded her way to the top of the *Inquisitor*'s food chain until she was comfortably settled in an office with a decent view, enjoying perks that she'd never dreamed of, and now she had nothing. Or next to nothing, anyway. Without a job, it wouldn't be long before the life that she had carefully and painstakingly built for herself would come tumbling down. Along with Saul's ominous voice, the sound of failure had rung so loudly in her ears that she'd almost broken down and cried like a baby.

Now, thank God, something else was ringing in her ears — the sound of a blazing comeback and the financial backing that she needed to make it happen. Then, as if on cue, Norman Harper's voice was in her ear.

"Miss Valentine, I've been looking forward to your call. . . ."

Hours later, Tressie's mind was whirling, trying to mentally prioritize the thousand and one details she had to deal with. With an open and half-packed suitcase on her bed, a confirmed travel itinerary in her hand and a big smile on her face, she raced around her apartment, checking to make sure that she wasn't forgetting anything important. By this time tomorrow she'd be a thousand miles away and, as far as she was concerned, in a whole other world. Nothing about where she was going was convenient or, for that matter, modern, so she wanted to make sure that she'd be able to exist with a modicum of comfort for the precious few days that she had to be there. She threw her makeup case into the suitcase and followed it up with as many pairs of Christian Louboutin pumps as it would take to see her through a week's visit, her laptop, a compact portable printer and a global Wi-Fi modem the size of a lipstick tube.

The essentials out of the way, she went in search of clothing.

It'd been five years since she'd stepped foot in Mercy, Georgia, and just thinking about going back almost wiped the smile right off her face. Only the possibility of finally acquiring something worthwhile from the dreary little town that she'd come from kept her feet moving and her mind clicking. If she felt the least bit guilty about selling her grandmother's house — the house that she had grown up in — well . . . she figured she'd get over it soon enough.

Hopefully.

CHAPTER 1

Not even the throwback R & B blaring from the earbuds in Tressie Valentine's ears could keep her energized long enough to get through the exhausting task of airing out and packing up Juanita Valentine's entire house in one afternoon. Her grandmother, who'd affectionately been called Ma'Dear by everyone who knew her, had collected all sorts of decorative knickknacks during her lifetime, and now there had to be hundreds of the little things scattered around the house. Each and every one of them was a dust magnet, and, unfortunately, Tressie had inherited all of them along with the house itself. If she'd had the energy to lift her leg, she would've kicked herself for letting the house sit unattended for the past five years. Even with the preliminary packing and tidying that she and some of Ma'Dear's lifelong friends had done after Ma'Dear's funeral, there was still a month's worth of work that had to be done in a fraction of that time.

The plan had been to get the second floor done, break for lunch and order a pizza for delivery, sit down and recuperate long enough to devour it, and then tackle the first floor. But when the muscles in her arms and legs threatened to revolt, she knew it was time to give it a rest. With the kitchen, dining room and living room still left to get through, she switched off her iPod, fixed herself a tall glass of ice water and took it with her out onto the back sunporch.

"God, even the porch furniture is dusty," she whined as she dropped into an ancient rocking chair and drank deeply. Her mental list of things to do was getting longer and longer. She hadn't dusted and cleaned so much since she was a teenager and now she remembered why. Ma'Dear had been the most loving grandmother that anyone could ask for, but she had also run a tight ship. As a teenager, most of Tressie's daily, weekly and monthly chores had revolved around housekeeping, which she had always detested, and Ma'Dear had stopped just short of following her around the house wearing a white glove to test for residue just to make sure that she was doing the cleaning correctly. When Tressie was first starting out on her own, far, far away from Mercy, house-work had been a necessary evil, but as soon as she'd been able to afford it she had hired a housekeeper and never looked back.

A moan slipped out of her mouth as she put her aching feet up on a nearby stool, let her head fall back against the chair and closed her eyes. It didn't help matters any that the temperature outside was at least ninety degrees. Inside the house it felt as if it was twice that, even with the windows wide-open and the electric fans that she'd found in the attic going full speed. After less than forty-eight hours in Mercy, Georgia, she suspected that she'd already lost at least five pounds just by virtue of sweating alone.

And she still had the downstairs to finish up.

Consolidated Investments, the firm that Norman Harper represented, wanted to take immediate possession of the house and the five acres of land that it sat on. She was scheduled to meet with him tomorrow afternoon to discuss terms and sign over the deed, and by then she was hoping to have everything in the house completely packed up and cleared out.

There wasn't much that she wanted to keep — just a few odds and ends. The rest she was going to donate to charity. As for the house itself . . . well, giving it up would be bittersweet, but she had to face facts. She never intended to live in Mercy again and she desperately needed the money. It didn't make sense for the house to continue sitting there like an unwanted and abandoned museum, or the land to go on being an unused burden on the town. As it was, she was itching to get back to New York and start reviving her career, and nothing here could help her do that.

Traffic to her online weblog had drastically fallen off in the months since her column had disappeared from the *Inquisitor.* Her website had once attracted nearly a million unique visitors daily, mostly because she had always reposted her print articles there, but there were also other tidbits and points of interest that drew attention. Fashion tips, popular high-end cosmetic and fragrance ad placements, updates on some of her favorite scandalous reality TV shows, exclusive celebrity interviews, and on and on. The kinds of stuff that interested women, which was her target audience, and kept them coming back for more. Just as she'd hoped, it hadn't taken the public long to notice her absence and sound off about it both on her blog and in the Letters to the

Editor section of the *Inquisitor.*

But the loyalty that she'd counted on had turned out to be a joke, and Saul was probably laughing his head off about it now. She could just see him, mumbling *I told you so*'s to anyone who'd listen, and comforting himself with the knowledge that he'd been right all along about her impulsiveness ultimately being her downfall.

Apparently, Vanessa Valentino was just another disposable commodity. After a few weeks' worth of inquiring comments, her audience had dropped her like a hot potato and moved on without a second thought. The blog was silent as a tomb now, which had initially struck like a blow straight to her heart, but the more she thought about it, the more she was beginning to feel that maybe it was for the best. When she did make her comeback — and she *would* make a comeback — she'd make that much more of a splash. Saul wouldn't be laughing then.

Ma'Dear had never completely understood what she did for a living, because Tressie had never really been completely forthcoming about her occupation. If there had ever been a Bible-thumping, God-fearing woman, it was Ma'Dear. She would've seen Tressie's occupation as a celebrity gossip columnist as a complete and

27

utter waste of God-given time. So Tressie had led Ma'Dear to believe that she was simply a staff reporter, a lowly one at that, who spent her workdays doing research and writing copy for the big-name reporters. If Ma'Dear had ever suspected that there was more to the story, thank God she'd never said so, because Tressie would've hated lying to the woman who had raised her after her mother had died in childbirth.

But she would've, in a heartbeat.

Fortunately, that was all behind her now. Ma'Dear was the only family that she'd had left in the world and she missed her every day, but without her to act as Tressie's long-distance conscience, Vanessa Valentino was free to take her game to the next level. And without Saul breathing down her neck and constantly trying to rein her in, she could expand her reach in ways that she'd been wanting to for years. Vanessa Valentino could finally become a brand name.

No, Vanessa Valentino *would* finally become a brand name. She had the contacts, the ideas and the guts to make it happen for herself. All she had to do now was get her hands on the money from the sale of the two things still tying her to Mercy, Georgia, by a thin thread — the house and land that Ma'Dear had left her.

Determined to meet the deadline that she had set for herself, Tressie forced herself to rise from the rocking chair and stretch her tired muscles. Suddenly starving, she deposited her empty glass in the kitchen sink and went in search of her cell phone. First she'd take a quick shower and then order lunch. Then she'd finish dealing with the house today if it was the last thing she did.

After an inexplicably delayed clearance from the airport in Darfur and then an excruciatingly long red-eye flight that was riddled with nonstop turbulence, all Nathaniel Woodberry wanted to do was make his way to the nearest bed and hibernate for at least the next twenty-four hours. But there was still an hour-long drive to look forward to once his flight landed in Atlanta and he finally made it through airport security. Fortunately, his bag was the first to appear on the luggage ramp and, thanks to his publicist, who also doubled as his personal assistant, a rented SUV was waiting for him at the valet station outside.

Already missing the love of his life — a vintage Jeep Wrangler that had seen just as much combat as he had — he tossed his gigantic duffel bag into the backseat of an idling Lincoln Navigator, peeled off his leather blazer and slid into the driver's seat. With the air-conditioning set to high, the radio tuned in to an all-jazz station and his cell phone switched off, he drove away from the airport and headed for the interstate and home.

For the past two decades he had called Seattle, Washington, home, but there was home and then there was *home*. Seattle was where he had settled right after graduating from college and accepting an entry-level staff reporter position with the *Seattle Times*. It was where he had gotten his start as a local news reporter and honed his craft — where he had fully indulged his photography hobby and invested in his first Nikon. Even back then his camera had pointed him toward chaos and controversy, which was how he'd found his twentysomething self wandering into the midst of an infamous Seattle riot and snapping a series of pictures that had ultimately catapulted him from staff reporter to frontline investigative journalist.

From there, his camera had taken him into the kinds of volatile and unpredictable situations that many journalists wouldn't even dream of going into, let alone getting up close and personal with — wars in the Middle East and Africa, the jungles of

South America, guerrilla soldier camps . . .
By now the list was endless.

Somewhere along the way he had earned
a reputation for being a daredevil. Probably
right around the time he had decided to
strike out on his own and become a
freelance journalist, Nate thought as he
picked up speed on the interstate, activated
the cruise control and relaxed back into the
plush leather seat. Some had thought him a
fool for wanting to make his own rules and
choose his own path, and others had pre-
dicted quick and brutal career suicide for
him. But he'd been just hungry enough, just
stubborn and fearless enough, to put both
himself and his camera in imminent danger
again and again for the sake of a story.

His pictures, the words he paired them
with and occasionally the sound bites that
he sometimes risked his life recording on
location — all had graced the covers of
magazines and newspapers around the
world and been featured on countless online
and television news outlets. Now his services
were so in demand that his publicist was
overworked and in need of a raise, and Nate
was lucky if he was able to carve out time
for a quick vacation here and there between
assignments.

It'd been months since he had actually

met with his publicist in person and even longer than that since he'd stepped foot inside his apartment in Seattle, and covering the aftermath of the conflict in Darfur was only partly to blame. Trips like these, trips back home to Mercy, Georgia, were the other half of the equation.

At the Mercy exit, Nate left the interstate and cruised along the two-lane service road that led into town. Traffic on the usually quiet and scenic road was heavier than usual, inching along in some spots and coming to a complete standstill in others. He passed a long stretch of farmland before the scenery opened up to clusters of residential communities and then a small industrial park. It was the same scenery that had always been there, except that now there was a new addition. Just past the industrial parks, new construction was going on, ground being broken and buildings leveled.

Seeing it caused a wrinkle of irritation to appear in the center of Nate's forehead. He knew without having to track its progress that it was heading straight toward Mercy, Georgia. Short of a miracle suddenly happening, in a matter of months those demolition crews would be destroying the entire town and leaving hundreds of displaced people in their wake. People who wouldn't be able to afford to live in the resort-style, luxury gated community that was slated to be built in its place. In political terms, it was called *eminent domain,* but as far as the people of Mercy were concerned it was theft, plain and simple.

Nate tended to agree.

When the Welcome to Mercy, Georgia, sign finally appeared on the side of the road up ahead, Nate picked up his cell phone from the passenger seat, turned it on and pressed a button to connect to his publicist. The phone on the other end had barely rung once before it was answered.

"It's about time you called," Julia Gustav said by way of greeting. "I was beginning to wonder if I should call the police and have an APB put out on you. Oh, but wait, I wouldn't be able to give them an accurate description of you, now, would I? God knows I haven't seen you in forever. Do you even care that I miss you?"

Nate chuckled, glad that Julia couldn't see him just then. He was blushing like a schoolboy, which was exactly what she made him feel like sometimes. "I know, sugar, and I'm sorry. It can't be helped right now, but I'll tell you what. How about I take you out for a night on the town when I get back to Seattle?" he said. "We'll take in a show, have a lavish dinner and drink bubbly all night. Maybe take a walk by the lakefront and catch up. Sound good?"

"Better than good," Julia purred. "Promise?"

"Of course. It'll be just like old times."

Julia had been his publicist and personal assistant for more than a decade, which meant that she knew him better than he knew himself most of the time. At sixty years old, she was the closest thing to a favorite aunt he'd ever had, and he was crazy about her. Ever since his mother had passed away six months ago, Julia had taken it upon herself to become his keeper, insisting that he call her at least once every other day, regardless of where he was in the world or what he was doing, just as he had called his mother. Normally, he was able to deliver, but being damn near undercover in Darfur, with limited or no cell access for hundreds of miles and very little human contact that hadn't required a translator, had kept him out of touch for longer than usual this time. It went without saying that he had some making up to do.

"No, it won't," Julia told him. "The last time we went out for a night on the town, your mother was with us." Her voice turned wistful. "You flew us both to New York on a private jet, like we were queens, and took us to a Broadway show. We sat next to that famous actress and her husband, and your mother couldn't believe that you were actually friends with them." Julia laughed throatily. "She had the best time."

"Yes, she did," Nate said quietly, remembering. Merlene Woodberry had been like a kid in a candy store whenever she visited New York, and her last trip there was no different. When she hadn't been dragging him around to every tourist attraction that the city had to offer, she'd spent hours on end walking him around Time Square, watching people and marveling at their antics. At the time, Nate had chalked up her hyperenthusiasm to the fact that she had decided that the trip would be her last for the next little while. She had more clients than normal back home, she'd said, and there were some things that she wanted to have done around the house that she needed to be home to oversee.

He'd had no idea that she was dying.

"So we'll dedicate the night to her memory," he suggested with a cheerfulness that he was nowhere near feeling. "She'd like that."

"Hmm, I think she would also approve of what you're trying to do for your hometown.

35

It's a special little place."

"It was to her."

His ancestors had lived in Mercy since the slaves were emancipated, and Merlene had lived and breathed the town. As for him — well, it had always been a nice place to live as long as he'd actually had to. But the minute he was old enough to start dreaming about places far, far away, he had started planning his escape route. Still, Mercy was special — Julia was right about that. His mother would never forgive him if he didn't at least try to save it.

Julia's voice broke into his thoughts. "So I'll see you in, what? A couple of days? A week?"

"Maybe a little longer. There's a town-hall meeting scheduled for tomorrow that I want to sit in on, and then I have a meeting the day after that. So we'll see how it goes."

After hanging up, Nate tossed his cell phone back into the passenger seat, only to have it ring again. He snatched it up again. "Woodberry."

"When you said you were coming home today, did you mean today or did you mean next month today?" a deep, gravelly voice asked.

He rolled his eyes to the roof of the car and took a breath for patience. "I'm driving into town as we speak, Jasper," he drawled. He rolled to a halt at the stoplight in front of the funeral home that Jasper Holmes owned and tooted his horn loud enough to be heard inside the three-story building. Jasper lived in the bachelor's apartment on the top floor. "Did you hear that, old man?"

"That you?"

"Yep. You need anything while I'm in the area?" If he'd ever had an uncle, which he hadn't, he probably would've been just like Jasper Holmes, Nate thought as he idled at the red light. Growing up, he had never quite cleaved to Jasper the way most of the town's kids had, seeing him as a surrogate father figure, but the two of them had always had a grudging respect for one another. "Dinner? Your medicine? An ass-kicking in dominoes?"

Jasper cackled heartily at the thinly veiled but good-natured threat. "You wish, boy. You wish. I might take you up on that tomorrow sometime, though. Right now I'm thinking about putting some ribs in the smoker out back. Hallie Norris called me this morning and said that Elaine Gordon told her that Jessie down at Hayden's Diner told her that Juanita Valentine's granddaughter popped up in town the other day. Jessie says she's been ordering takeout from the diner morning, noon and night, and we both know how Willie Burnett's cooking can burn a hole in your gut. So I figured I might smoke a few pieces of meat, whip up some potato salad and see if I could talk Lilly Davis into throwing some stuff into a pot and ending up with her version of spaghetti. Figured the least we could do is feed the girl. Juanita was good people. She —"

Nate hadn't listened to a word Jasper had said past hearing that Juanita Valentine's granddaughter was in town. "Wait a minute. Did you just say that Tressie Valentine is in town?"

"Yeah," Jasper confirmed. "Been here since the day before yesterday, the way I hear it. She's staying in Juanita's house. Well, I guess it's her house now, but —"

"Do me a favor and hold up on setting out a buffet, okay? Let me look into some things and I'll call you back."

Nate disconnected the call and made a U-turn on two wheels in the middle of Main Street. Ignoring the blaring horns of drivers who had been suddenly and illegally cut off, he drove back the way he had come. Less than a hundred feet from the Welcome to Mercy, Georgia, sign at the entrance to town and directly across the street from the Greyhound bus station was a one-way road

38

that circled around to the east side of town and opened up to a small cluster of residential streets. The area ran alongside a dense, wooded thatch and, years ago, it had been separated from the rest of the town by wrought-iron gates at each end. The houses inside the gates were the largest in Mercy, rambling three- and four-story structures that only the handful of wealthy residents in Mercy could afford to own. Beyond it, up on the hill, was the house that he and all of the other kids in Mercy had fondly referred to as the White House. Before the gates had been taken down, the farthest that he had ventured inside the gates had been to occasionally visit Moira Tobias, the owner of the White House. Now he made a beeline for another house, the one that Tressie Valentine had grown up in with her grandmother.

Nate skidded to a stop behind the small sedan that was parked in the driveway and hopped out of the Navigator before the machine had fully registered the shift from Drive to Park. It was still shuddering when he took the steps leading to the wraparound front porch two at a time and rang the doorbell.

Thirty seconds later and no response, he rang the doorbell again. Then again. Still no response. Cursing under his breath, he tried the doorknob. His eyebrows shot up in surprise when it turned easily and the door swung open.

The first floor was clear, he discovered after checking out each room. Other than stacks of already packed boxes and flattened boxes waiting to be packed scattered everywhere, there was no sign of Tressie. He was wondering if she had gone out somewhere when he heard sounds of movement above his head. Exactly what the source of those sounds was didn't register with him until he was already on the second floor and approaching the first door to his left — the door to the hall bathroom.

The shower.

It was going full blast and she was singing along with the water's spray. No, that wasn't quite right. Actually she was singing — horribly — over and above the water's spray. The sound of her voice scraped across his nerves like fingernails on a chalkboard, spiking his irritation level into orbit. Without stopping to think about what he was doing, he barged into the steamy bathroom and snatched the shower curtain back.

"What the hell are you doing here?" he bellowed.

Chapter 2

She turned just as a blast of cool air slammed into her skin, and then visions of warriors rushing in for battle flashed before her eyes — big, strapping men with bulging muscles, bloodthirsty expressions on their faces, and mighty swords slicing through the air. She saw herself being impaled to death and then buried in a shallow grave deep in the woods, where no one would ever find her. She saw, as plain as day, the likelihood that no one would even bother to look for her because the sad fact was that she wasn't the most popular person in the world and she had no real friends to speak of. Every questionable deed that she'd ever done played before her eyes like a movie. Her killer would go unpunished and her death would be in vain. The public would probably celebrate once her true identity was revealed. They would —

Oh, God. She was going to die.

Partially blinded by soap bubbles and completely on the verge of hysteria, Tressie opened her mouth and did the only thing she could think to do under the circumstances. She screamed at the top of her lungs.

It seemed like an eternity, but it really took only a few seconds to wipe the soap bubbles from her eyes and focus. When she did, the first thing she saw through the steam was a pair of gorgeous hazel eyes staring into hers. Expanding her gaze to a wide-screen view, she took in a pair of perfectly shaped lips and a dimpled chin, thick eyebrows and smooth pecan-brown skin. Something in her brain eventually clicked and she recognized Nate Woodberry, but that didn't stop her from continuing to scream like a banshee. The only difference was that this time the sounds she made were intelligible. "What the hell," she shrieked frantically as she snatched the shower curtain from his grasp and wrapped it around her body, "are you doing in here?"

"I rang the bell. You didn't answer." He was the epitome of calm.

"So you just walk right on in and make yourself at home?" She slung her wet hair back and out of her face and shut off the water. "Idiot! Hand me a towel from over there, would you?" She snatched the towel he handed her and only released her death grip on the shower curtain long enough to make the trade. The fact that he had undoubtedly seen more of her naked body in the past thirty seconds than her doctor had in years burned her skin to a cherry-red crisp, especially since he hadn't so much as given it a second glance in all that time. So much for cutting back on sweets and working out like a demon.

"Well?" they said in unison.

"Well, what?" they said in harmony again.

And then again in unison, "What are you doing here?"

"You first," Tressie said, securing the knot in her towel and stepping out of the old-fashioned claw-foot tub.

"No, sugar, you first." Nate folded his arms across his chest and stared her down. "You were told to stay the hell away from Mercy, Georgia, but yet here you are. Why is that, *Vanessa Valentino*?"

She resisted the urge to wince at the menacing way he said her trade name. Of the handful of people who knew that she was the pen behind the persona, unfortunately he had always been the least complimentary about it. "I'm sorry. Did I miss the memo that named you the king of my comings and goings?" She folded her arms underneath her breasts and looked at him from head to toe, then rolled her eyes. "Just because you had a bug up your ass about a story I was writing five years ago doesn't mean you can order me around for the rest of my life. News flash, Nate. It was a long time ago. The rest of the world has moved on. You should, too."

"What, you think I've spent the last five years checking for you?"

"Well, you are standing in my bathroom right now, aren't you?" She looked up at him thoughtfully. "Tell me something, Nate. How did you even know that I was here? Which one of your little minions do you have keeping track of my every movement?"

He caught his mouth before it could drop open. "You're out of your mind."

"Says the man who's hunted me down like a fugitive for the second time in less than a decade."

"You are a fugitive."

Now it was her turn to catch her mouth before it could drop open. "Excuse me?"

"That's what you do, right? Hide behind a fake name and a fake persona so you don't have to face the consequences of destroying people's lives with the stroke of a pen? That's you, right? A hack, so-called journalist, with nothing better to do than dig around in people's private lives, because you have no life of your own? A coward who throws stones and then hides her hands? If the public knew who you really were, you'd never get another night's sleep."

Almost word for word, he was spouting the same speech now that he had given her five years ago, except that he wasn't shouting the roof off this time. She didn't know which was worse — enraged and volatile Nate, or the calm, almost reasonable-sounding Nate standing in front of her now. Either way, she wasn't in the mood for a replay of five years ago, especially since she hadn't exactly come out on top in the aftermath. Every time she thought about the way she had allowed him to bully her into dropping the story of a lifetime — and she had thought about it a lot over the years — she wanted to kick herself. If she had held her ground back then she would've been a wealthy woman right now. More than wealthy, she thought sourly. Probably rich. And none of the chaos that was currently going on in her life would be happening.

Was she pissed at the way things had turned out? Hell, yes.

Had she stood there five years ago like a deer caught in headlights and allowed Nate to insult her nonstop? Yes, she had.

That was then and this was now. He had won back then, and there was nothing she could do about that now. She wasn't about to let him terrorize her again. She had too much riding on this visit to Mercy and, thankfully, it had nothing to do with him.

But just to be on the safe side, she took a full step back from him before throwing one of the stones he'd mentioned. "You know, it's funny that you mention me not having a life, when you're the one who's dedicated his entire life to chasing after another man's woman. Where's the dignity in that, Nate, huh?"

He went stone still and his eyes narrowed. "I have no idea what you're talking about," he said quietly.

Shut up, Tressie. Shut up now. "Oh, of course you do. I was here back then, too, remember? You were so in love with Pamela Mayes that you couldn't see straight. Always trailing behind her and her boyfriend, hoping she would throw you a scrap of attention whenever she happened to look around and notice you there. But she never did, did she? What was his name? The boy she chose over you? Oh, that's right. Chad Greene. Your *best friend.* Some friend you are."

"Watch yourself, Tressie."

"It was a sordid little story for a while there, and isn't it a shame that I didn't get to tell it."

"You didn't need to tell it. It was none of your business."

"Whatever," Tressie snapped, flapping a dismissive hand at him. "Like I said, it was five years ago. I kept up my end of the deal, so what do you want with me now?" The deal. Just thinking about it put a sour taste in her mouth.

When he had shown up at her office at the *Inquisitor,* some obviously delusional part of her mind had actually thought that he was there to invite her out to lunch or, even better, dinner. True, they didn't exactly run in the same journalistic circles, but they had just run into each other in Mercy, when she had gone home for Ma'Dear's funeral, and the vibe between them had been good. At least she'd thought so. Apparently her radar for gauging a man's interest was seriously out of order, because not only couldn't he have been less interested in taking her out to dinner, but he'd been on the verge of shaking her silly.

Accusations had been hurled and the shouting had been almost unbearable, and that was just on his part. For her part, she'd barely been able to get a word in. By the

47

time he had calmed down long enough to issue a parting ultimatum, she'd been in tears. Drop the story, he'd said, or get ready for the world to know who she really was. It would've been a career-ending move, and no matter how badly she wanted to write columns that would bring the public to its knees, she couldn't risk it.

And he'd known that.

Bastard.

"I want you not to make me take you to the mat again," Nate said ominously. "Because you know I will."

"For what?" Disbelief had her rearing back and staring up at him as if he was crazy, which very likely could've been the case. Studies had shown that some of the most attractive men in history had been quietly, secretly insane, and Nate Woodberry was way beyond attractive. He was tall and wrapped from head to toe in the kind of muscle that couldn't be earned in a gym, and his smile, whenever he was moved to reveal it, which wasn't very often it seemed, was just lopsided enough, just devilish enough to conjure up images of all kinds of X-rated deeds. His hair, when it wasn't secured at the nape of his neck in a roguish ponytail, was an inky black curtain that draped his shoulders and hung down his back in silky waves. And when they weren't narrowed to slits, his hazel eyes were sleepy-looking, as if he had just rolled out of bed. Any woman with a pulse would be tempted to roll him right back into bed upon first sight of him. Love didn't immediately come to mind when you set eyes on him, but pure and simple lust damn sure did.

Quite frankly, he was a spectacular-looking man, which meant that the odds of his being completely off his rocker were greater than most. And here she was, naked except for a wash-worn towel and all alone with him in a nearly soundproof house. The way things were going, he could snap any second now, and what could she do? Beat him off with a towel that was probably just as old as she was?

"You know what?" Tressie said, mentally switching gears and frantically shooing him out of her way. "Forget I asked. I can't deal with you right now, so I think it's time for you to go." She was surprised when he actually stepped aside, but she wasn't about to waste a second of precious time thanking him. As soon as the way was clear, she made a beeline for the open door and the hallway on the other side of it. The bedroom she was using was directly across from the bathroom. Gripping her towel and walking fast, she headed toward it, praying every step of the way.

Walking just as fast behind her, Nate cuffed her arm and brought her skipping back to him two steps shy of her goal. "Just a second, sugar. I want to make sure we're clear on something before you go back into hiding." He dipped his head and put his face in her face. "Are you listening?"

Momentarily thrown off balance by the sheer impact of him, Tressie couldn't find her voice. Good lord, the man was even more gorgeous up close. Some other part of her brain, some irrational, hypersexual part, wondered what he would do if she closed the inch separating his lips from hers and sucked his bottom lip into her mouth. *Just curious,* she'd say when he asked her what the hell she thought she was doing. Did he taste as good as he looked? Inquiring, sexually deprived minds suddenly wanted to know.

Pamela Mayes would know, she thought as her stricken gaze made its way down to the lips in question. Nate had been romantically linked to hundreds of high-profile women over the years, and somehow none of them had ever managed to drag him down the aisle. Whenever the topic of his lingering bachelorhood had come up in any of the personal interviews that he sometimes came out of seclusion and granted, he'd always rattled off some nonsense about not having found the right woman yet. But Tressie knew better. He had found the right woman years ago and let her slip through his fingers. All the other women that he'd romanced had just been extremely well-endowed, picture-perfect substitutes.

That information alone would've guaranteed sales in the hundreds of thousands if she'd been allowed to write even a fraction of the story.

Pamela Mayes was a country girl turned mega-superstar. She had turned her humble beginnings as an orphan here in Mercy, Georgia, into platinum records and multiple Grammy awards, stints on reality TV shows and, just this past year, a series of designer fragrances and a new makeup line. She was a household name, having been compared to legendary songbirds such as Whitney Houston and Mariah Carey when it came to vocal style and ability, and hottie newcomer celebrities like Jennifer Lopez and Kim Kardashian when it came to the scandal factor. As a result, the public loved her and the media dogged her every move.

Nate wasn't an entertainer in the common sense of the word, but he was just as much a celebrity as Pamela Mayes was. As a reporter at a well-respected news station, he had established what would've ended up being a respectable, if not mundane, career for himself. But as a freelance investigative journalist, he had found a way not only to entertain people, but also to make them think. If his stories were informative, sometimes hard to swallow and often gut-wrenching, the photos that he took, the magic that he created from behind the lens, were absolutely awe-inspiring and even more so. He took the pictures that others turned away from and made you look at them. It hadn't taken the powers that be long to notice that special something that he possessed, and along with notoriety had come wealth and a different kind of fame. On top of that, he was mouthwateringly sexy.

Linking him with Pamela Mayes and being able to substantiate the link with the kind of factual evidence that Tressie could've provided would have ignited her career. And then writing a no-holds-barred follow-up exposé about the life and times of the infamous Pamela Mayes, about everything that happened before and after her relationship with Nate Woodberry, would've shot Tressie's career straight into orbit.

But she had missed the boat and now it was too late.

The trauma of burying her twin sister, the only biological family that Pam ever had, had already been written about in a biography that had sold millions of copies while Tressie had been too afraid to defy Nate's order of silence. Pam had been involved in other scandals since then, and now that she was happily married and fairly domesticated, she was busy trying to build a legacy that she could be proud of. These days she was working hard to downplay her penchant for negative media attention and bring her philanthropic efforts to the forefront.

So Tressie would never get to write about what had to have been an intense connection between Nate and Pam. They had been lovers — she was sure of it, though she didn't have a scrap of proof. Nate would never admit to it and Pam wasn't exactly in a position to be completely forthcoming, but there it was just the same.

As if reading her thoughts, Nate's lips moved closer and hovered less than a breath away from hers. "I can see that you are listening," he whispered, "so I'll make this quick. To answer your question, sugar — no, I'm not the king of your comings and goings. No man in his right mind would want that responsibility. But for the next little while, let's just say that I'm the king of Mercy, Georgia, and as the king, I'm giving you a royal decree. If you came here to stick your pointy little nose into the eminent domain situation here in Mercy and make a mockery of it, forget about it. These people need help, but they don't need your kind of help. Understood?"

No, but . . . whatever. "Um, yeah, I guess so."

"Good. Do you need me to help you pack?"

"N-no." Especially since she wasn't planning on going anywhere.

"Then we understand each other."

"Perfectly."

"Good. So I'll see myself out."

"Please do."

Silly man, Tressie thought as she watched Nate disappear down the stairs. Now that he had piqued her curiosity, did he really think she was going to just pack up and leave without finding out what was going on?

She breathed a sigh of relief when she heard the door slam and then raced downstairs to the front door to double lock it behind him. Back upstairs, she went into her old bedroom and peeked out the window at him from behind the blinds. The Navigator burned rubber backing out of the driveway and taking off down the street. Once it was out of sight, she dropped her towel and slipped into a pair of shorts and a fresh tank top.

Then she powered up her laptop and went on a searching expedition. An eminent domain situation in Mercy, Georgia? What the hell?

The Navigator couldn't carry Nate away from Tressie's house fast enough. Pushing the bulky machine well beyond posted speed limits, he drove back the way he had come by rote, his thoughts churning at warp speed despite the fact that his body was exhausted. Before he had discovered that Tressie was back in town, all he had wanted to do was get to his mother's house as quickly as possible, take a long, hot shower and crawl into bed. Now all he could think about was seeing Tressie naked, and suddenly the prospect of getting into an empty bed didn't seem quite so satisfying.

He hadn't been intimate with a woman in several months, almost a year by his own self-imposed-celibacy calculations, and he was feeling deprived of it right now more than ever. When he was on assignment, the story always took precedence. Women, as much as he loved them, were a luxury that he couldn't afford to indulge in. The slightest distraction on location could cost him his life, so he had long since learned to channel all his energy in the only direction that mattered — time and place, and getting in and out alive.

The press liked to paint a picture of him that was far from the reality of his everyday life. For every woman that he'd ever actually established some sort of relationship with, there were at least ten more that they had erroneously linked him to. If he let them tell it, he spent most of his time seducing unsuspecting women and breaking their hearts. But the exact opposite was actually closer to the truth. When he wasn't on location, he spent most of his time locked away in his darkroom, which was precisely why none of the relationships that he had taken time out of his busy schedule to cultivate had ever actually moved past the dating stage.

He was married to his work.

But he wasn't working now and, with images of Tressie's water-streaked breasts etched into his brain, his body was acutely aware of exactly how long it'd been since he had been close enough to a woman to do anything more than breathe in her scent. Not that he was the least bit interested in Tressie Valentine, he reminded himself as he executed a left turn that balanced the Navigator on two wheels, because he wasn't. Still, he couldn't help wondering how he'd never noticed that she was so damn sexy.

Of course, the possibility that he was half-out of his mind from lack of sex was a very real one. But he was pretty sure that he'd been thinking with the right head when he noticed that her bottom lip was slightly plumper than her top one and, therefore, begging to be sucked; that she had twin beauty marks — one centered perfectly above her top lip and the other in the center of her chin — and he'd thought about touching the tip of his tongue to them. That her breasts were beautifully tipped with what had looked to his suddenly dry mouth like large, ripe blackberries. Hadn't he?

Either way it was a moot point because Tressie Valentine had to be the last person on earth that he wanted to get involved with, even if it would've been just for the sake of hot, sweaty sex. For one thing, she talked too much and he had never been attracted to chatty women. And for another, he wasn't inclined to deal with the kind of drama that she would undoubtedly introduce into his life. His hands were full enough as it was with the drama going on in Mercy, without adding another ingredient to the mix. Plus, if there was a God in heaven, the woman would be on the other side of the state line, headed back to New York, before nightfall.

Pushing any and all thoughts of Tressie Valentine to the back of his mind, Nate pulled into his own driveway and shut off the Navigator. As he hauled his duffel into the house and took it with him into the only room in the house that was still furnished, he decided that if she wasn't gone by the end of the day, he would track her down — again — and strangle the hell out of her.

CHAPTER 3

If there was one good thing about committing a crime in Mercy, Georgia, Tressie told herself as she raised a window at the back of Nate's house and hiked up her sundress so she could climb inside, it was that people never locked their windows or doors. The rest of the world had moved on to high-tech alarm systems, vicious guard dogs and megawatt floodlights, but not Mercy. The crime rate here was next to nothing, which made it way too easy for people like her to do exactly what she was doing — breaking and entering.

At the last minute, she remembered that she was wearing stilettos and took them off before she tucked her miniflashlight between her teeth, boosted herself up on the window ledge and dove through the window like a cat. Inside, she landed as quietly as she could on her elbows and knees, and quickly scrambled to her feet. The kitchen was clear, as was the hallway beyond it and what she could see of the living room.

She stood still for a second, listening to the sounds of the house and waiting for her eyes to adjust to the darkness. Somewhere a clock was ticking and the central air-conditioning unit was humming steadily, but otherwise not a creature seemed to be stirring. She knew that Nate was home, because the Navigator that he'd been driving earlier was parked in the driveway. Leaving her shoes on the floor by the window, she inched forward and crept deeper into the house on the tips of her toes.

In the living room, she moved across the hardwood floor stealthily, being careful not to trip the built-in alarm in the center of the room. The slight dip in the wood there was invisible to the naked eye, but anyone who had ever come to Miss Merlene for a press-and-curl back in the day knew exactly where it was. At three o'clock in the afternoon, the loud squeal that it emitted was tolerable, but at three o'clock in the morning, it definitely wasn't the kind of entrance that Tressie wanted to make. She breathed a silent sigh of relief when she made it to the other side of the room and then to the short hallway that led to the bedrooms without making a sound.

After that, finding Nate was a piece of cake. She killed the flashlight and followed the dim glow of the night-light that he'd left on in the bathroom adjoining his bedroom. He was in bed, sleeping wildly with the bedspread kicked back and off him, a pillow bunched underneath his head and a sheet wound around his waist. One of his legs lay on top of the sheet and an arm hung off the side of the huge bed. Setting her flashlight on the nightstand, Tressie moved closer to the sleeping giant.

"Nate," she whispered. The steady rise and fall of his chest continued undisturbed. She tried again, a little louder this time. "Nate!" Still nothing. Carefully sidestepping his dangling arm, she leaned over him and slowly reached out. "Nate."

Even in sleep the man was a god. Long-limbed and artfully sculpted, he was like a carved, life-size sex toy, Tressie decided as her gaze wandered south and followed the trail of fine, dark hair that began at his navel and snaked down his abdomen until it disappeared beneath the sheet. She was tempted to touch him there, just to see if the hair was as soft and springy as it looked, but she settled for touching the warm, smooth skin on his shoulder instead.

"Nate, wake up." A deep, throaty groan

was the only indication that he'd heard her.

"Nate, wake up." She shook him softly. "It's me, Tressie. I need to talk to you. Wake up." Several seconds passed before it finally occurred to her that he was nowhere near the waking point. As if she needed further convincing, he stirred just long enough to stretch languidly, push one hand up and underneath the pillow he was lying on, and then push the other one down and underneath the sheet pooled around his waist. Willing herself not to think about what he was possibly touching down there, she leaned over Nate and flattened a hand on his chest. "Dammit, Nate. Wake up, would you?"

He twitched and she jumped. Then he settled back into sleep again, and she pressed a hand to her chest to steady her pounding heart. He twitched again and she held her breath, waiting. As it turned out, she didn't have to wait long.

"Oh, my God" was all she had the presence of mind to say when he sprang toward her like a cobra. The next thing she knew, she was airborne and screaming, once again, at the top of her lungs.

Goddamned woman, Nate thought as he hauled her lithe and protesting little body across the bed and rolled with her. She was scrambling to get her bearings, but her flailing arms and legs were no match for the element of surprise. No doubt he had scared the hell out of her, but from where he was lying, turnabout was fair play. Waking up in the middle of the night to find someone lurking in the dark, standing over him with, as far as he was concerned, questionable intentions, hadn't exactly done his heart any good, either.

She landed on her back in the middle of the bed and he came down on top of her, thinking the entire time about shaking her until her teeth rattled. She was like a fly. The more you swatted at the damn thing, the more it kept buzzing around your head. But even flies got the hint after a while. What the hell was she still doing in Mercy?

His hands found hers and clamped them to the mattress above her head before she could scratch his eyes out or worse, and his knee wedged its way between hers . . . just in case. She was still screaming her head off, but he wasn't about to release one of her hands so that he could cover her mouth.

"Would you please shut up?" Nate growled in Tressie's ear. "You know damn well who I am and where you are."

As if someone had flipped a switch, Tressie

fell silent. A second later, she giggled. "Of course I know it's you. I snuck in here, remember?"

"Which begs the obvious question — why?"

Chest-to-chest and face-to-face, they stared at each other.

"Because I thought it would add an air of mystery and suspense to the situation," she quipped, still giggling. "Plus, it was fun, sort of like riding a roller coaster. And you know what? Something tells me that you would be one hell of a roller-coaster ride, Nate."

"And something tells me that you need to have your head checked." Or maybe he was the one who needed his head checked. He had half a mind to throw her right back out the window that she had undoubtedly crawled through. The problem was the other half of his mind was wondering if the skin between her breasts, both of which were crushed between them like twin pillows at this very moment, smelled as good as the skin in the hollow of her neck did. Either too many forays into jungles and deserts were causing him to lose his mind, or she was some kind of witch doctor trying to cast a voodoo spell on him. When his penis perked up and started thinking with a mind of its own, he decided that it had to be the latter. "Give me one good reason why I shouldn't call the police and have you hauled off to jail?"

"Because it would be morning before they got here, and I don't have that long to wait," she said simply. As if she was just now realizing that he had her pinned down, she pulled at the viselike grip that he had on her hands and sighed when she couldn't move them. "Listen, would you mind letting go of my hands? Believe it or not, I didn't come here to wrestle with you."

"I learned a long time ago not to believe anything that comes out of your mouth," he sniped. But he rolled off her anyway. He grabbed the sheet and took it with him when he sat up on the side of the bed, hoping like hell that the erection jutting from between his thighs would relax and go back to sleep. "What could you possibly want at three o'clock in the morning?" he asked, staring at the alarm clock on the bedside table.

"I needed to talk to you." He heard her scrambling around behind him on the bed. Then her bare legs swung over the side of the bed next to his. He stared at the muscles in her calves as though he had never seen any before. "I did some checking after you left and —"

"Some checking?" His eyes changed direction and narrowed on her face. "Checking into what?"

"The eminent domain situation here in Mercy," she said as if he was a little mixed up in the head. "I didn't find much, which really surprised me. These kinds of stories usually make good community-relations pieces. As a journalist, I —"

He snorted.

Rolling her eyes, Tressie continued as if she hadn't heard the veiled insult. "*As a journalist,* the issue started me to thinking."

"This ought to be good," Nate drawled, pushing up from the bed and dragging the sheet along with him to the bathroom. A quick, cold shower was definitely in order. He rolled his eyes to the ceiling and stifled a groan when he heard Tressie following him. "Do you mind? I'm about to take a shower."

"Of course not. What's a couple of showers between old friends?" she chirped cheerfully. "I'll just come with you and talk loud so you can hear me over the water."

"I suppose this is payback for what happened earlier today," he said as he dropped the sheet and stepped into the shower. To hell with it — if she refused to give him some privacy, then she deserved the consequences. His penis was still standing at semi-attention when he turned on the water and adjusted the spray, still bobbing proudly in the air when she glanced down at it and froze comically. It took a few seconds for her gaze to rise above his waist and find his, and when it did it was decidedly feline. "I've seen you and you've seen me. Now we're even. Talk," he barked and then closed the glass shower door in her shocked face.

Luckily for her, Tressie recovered quickly. "Well, the way I see it, Mercy deserves a hell of a lot more media coverage than it's gotten so far," she began. "I had no idea that all this was going on down here. A couple of weeks ago, I got a letter from this company —"

"Consolidated Investments," he cut in.

"How did you know?"

"Lucky guess. Go on." Through the glass he saw that she had made a seat for herself on top of the vanity and had crossed her legs Indian-style. Her sundress was pooled around her hips, and every glorious inch of her legs was on display. An image of those legs wrapped around his neck streaked through his mind before he could stop it, and all he could do in its wake was grin humorlessly. Was this what he had been reduced to? Lusting against his will after a woman that couldn't have been less his type if she tried? She was curvy and voluptuous, and he had always preferred long and willowy. She was short, and tall was what usually caught his eye. She was energetic and bubbly, and laid-back was more his style. She giggled, and he had always liked the sound of a woman's slow, smoky laugh.

She was Vanessa Valentino, and he had added her name to his list of enemies five years ago.

"Right," she said. "They offered to buy the house and land that Ma'Dear left me, and the price was right so I figured, why not? Then you showed up and I knew there was more to the story. So I went digging."

He thought he already had a pretty good idea, but he asked anyway. "What did you find?"

"Almost nothing. Gwinnet County had a small blurb about the town-hall meeting tomorrow evening hidden in the back of the Community News section of their newspaper, and I found a public notice article that one of their reporters wrote a few months ago. According to the article, as soon as the town's charter expired back in March, Gwinnet County assumed guardianship of the town. Seems like thirty seconds later, they were in negotiations with Consolidated Investments to sell the town off. Who does that?" Without waiting for a response, she hopped down from the vanity and crossed the bathroom to open the shower door. "I've been thinking about it all day, Nate, and at first I couldn't quite put my finger on what it was about the situation that really bothered me. Then it came to me, and so I decided to come to you." She took a deep breath and squared her shoulders. "I smell a conspiracy and I know you do, too. Otherwise you wouldn't be here. You'd be off in Africa or the Middle East somewhere. What I want to know is, why haven't you done anything about it?"

He emerged from underneath the water's spray and pushed his fingers through his hair to slick it back from his face. "I'm working on it" was all he said.

"Oh. I guess you want a towel, huh?"

"That would be nice, yes." Otherwise he'd be hard as a rock again in no time flat and thinking with that head instead of the one on his shoulders. *She's not your type,* he reminded himself as his eyes watched her butt make its way over to the towel rack. She wasn't, but her backside begged to differ. As big as his hands were, he thought he could fill his palms with her ass and still leave a little in reserve. Then wrap his hands around her waist and feel the tips of his fingers meet with room to spare. She was curvy and ripe, with impossibly long legs and muscular thighs, but she was a tiny little thing.

No, she wasn't his type, but that didn't stop him from flirting with the thought of tossing her up onto the vanity, spreading her legs east and west, and losing himself inside her.

What would she do if he did?

She grabbed the first towel she saw, which was a hand towel that would barely cover his genitals, and tossed it at him. "Here. Soooo . . . okay, good. You're working on it." An ecstatic laugh bubbled out of her mouth, then she put a serious expression on her face and sobered up. "Here's the thing, though. You're going to need help and I want in," she said.

He looked at the towel and then at her. She looked so hopeful, so excited, that he almost felt sorry for her and caved in. But common sense prevailed at the last minute, enabling him to see past her sparkling brown eyes and pouty lips and come to the only conclusion that made sense. "Absolutely not," he said with finality.

"Oh, come on, Nate!"

"Hell, no."

"Naaate," she whined and stamped her foot, and for some inexplicable reason his penis stirred.

"No, and that's my final answer." He snatched his robe from a hook on the back of the bathroom door and yanked it on as he walked out of the bathroom.

Tressie was right behind him, hurrying along after him as he stalked through the dark house like a prowling panther. "This could be a win-win situation and you know it."

"It could also be a train wreck," he suggested calmly. He switched on the kitchen light and stopped short, eyeing the scene before him. He took in the open window, the bunched rug beneath it and the abandoned red-bottomed stilettos, then slanted Tressie a look over his shoulder that should've singed her skin. "This just proves my point," he said, heading for the coffeemaker. "Every move you make is always a half step away from criminality. Every move I make, on the other hand, is what journalism is all about."

"I get the job done," Tressie defended as she crossed the room and came to stand next to him at the counter. "There's something to be said for that."

"Your methods are beyond questionable."

Anticipating him, she opened a nearby cabinet, spotted a stack of coffee filters and passed them to him. A tingle of awareness shot up her arm when his fingers brushed hers, but she ignored it in favor of making her case. She could think about how seeing him naked had scattered her system later, when she was alone. "I prefer to call them *effective.*"

"Don't you have to get back to New York soon?"

"Nope." The look of disappointment on his face was priceless, almost funny, but she wouldn't let herself crack a smile. "I can stay here as long as you need me to."

His eyebrows shot up at that. "You mean you finally got fired from your job or, better yet, run out of New York."

"Not exactly," Tressie hedged. "Let's just say that I'm on hiatus for a little while." His expression went from hopeful to dubious in two seconds flat, and she flushed guiltily before she could check herself. "Okay, so maybe I got suspended." A wrinkle appeared in the center of his forehead. "All right, all right, suspended indefinitely. Look, the point is I need this story. I need the credibility that it'll give me. I'll finally be able to break away from the *Inquisitor* and go out on my own."

As if he hadn't heard her, Nate went about the business of brewing coffee. It wasn't looking good for her, Tressie thought nervously. Her first clue was when he took down one mug instead of two from the cabinet. Her second was when he picked up her shoes from the floor and handed them to her with a pointed look. She took them. What else could she do? But she had no intention of putting them on and climbing back out the window. Not until she got what she wanted, anyway.

She leaned against the counter and folded her arms underneath her breasts. "You know, if you think about it, you owe me this, Nate."

Clearly surprised, he froze in the midst of dumping heaping spoonfuls of powdered creamer into his mug, his hazel eyes narrowing on her face suspiciously. "Come again?"

"Five years ago, you asked me to do something for you and I did it." She held up a hand for silence when he would've protested. "Any way you want to spin it, the bottom line is that I did it. Now I'm asking you to do something for me, and I think you owe it to me to do it." She knew she'd made a dent in his armor when he let out a long, winding breath and scratched his fingers through his wet hair. Out of the corner of his eye, he caught her staring up at him, and he shook his head sadly.

"It would never work." He tried to sound resolute, but Tressie caught the hint of surrender in his voice that he couldn't hide. "We'd be at each other's throats every minute of the day. I can't work like that. I *don't* work like that. And, contrary to what you might believe, I definitely don't need an assistant."

"Why would we be at each other's throats?" The very idea was ridiculous. The only source of possible conflict between them that she could think of had to do with one thing and one thing only — sexual attraction. It didn't take a genius to figure out that something was brewing between them, but to her way of thinking, there was a very obvious and satisfactory solution to the problem — sex. If they did it right, and something told her that they would, it could very well end up being the perfect professional partnership. "Oh, you mean because we like what we see when we look at one another?" He looked as though he was about to say something and then thought better of it. Instead, he chuckled under his breath. "You didn't think I noticed, did you?

Well, I did, and you know what? It's so not a big deal. I mean, once we do it nonstop for a couple of days, and get it out of our systems, it'll be a nonissue."

He choked on a mouthful of coffee and she patted his back helpfully.

"That's why you're thinking we'd be at each other's throats, right? This . . ." She gestured wildly from him to her and then from her to him. "This curiosity between us or whatever it is? That should be easy enough to deal with. We're both adults. We know what we have to do. Sleep together and get it over with. It's a simple enough solution."

Breathing steadily now, he brought the steaming coffee mug to his mouth again and locked gazes with her over the rim. Took a cautious sip and swallowed slowly. "Like I said, you're out of your mind."

"What, are you afraid of me?"

He chuckled again. "I won't even dignify that with an answer."

"Well, then, what is it? You can't possibly still be holding a grudge against me for wanting to write a story about Pamela Mayes five years ago. Because if you are, you need to get over it and let me help you with this. You owe me, Nate."

Several seconds of silence passed and then

a full minute. And then another minute and he still hadn't said a word. When five minutes had passed and he had only looked away from her long enough to refresh his coffee and add more creamer, she gave in to the desperation she felt.

"I did a story on Gary Price and I guess I went a little too far this time, so I got suspended."

"Indefinitely," he reminded her. "And I'm guessing, without pay. That's why you need to sell your house and land."

"Yes."

"You'd be selling to the enemy. Consolidated Investments is in bed with Gwinnet County executives."

"I won't have much of a choice if nothing else comes along."

"Well, there's no pay associated with this story," Nate advised. "I'm doing this strictly pro bono, which means you would be, too. Whatever money problems you're having now, you'll still have them when this ends . . . however it ends."

"I understand that." *Don't get too excited, Tressie. Don't. Get. Excited.*

"And there are a few other things you should know," he began slowly. "First, we do this my way or you're out. None of your circus sideshow Vanessa Valentino antics.

You already know who and what I am. I don't do compromising situations or sensationalism. You jeopardize my reputation in any way and I will bury you. Got it?"

That was kind of harsh, she thought, but didn't dare say. She was perfectly content to let him think that he was in charge. "Got it." For now. "What about copy? Have you started writing any?"

He shook his head and took another sip of coffee. "Not yet. You can help with that if you like. I have started a photo journal, though."

"Pictures? You have pictures?" Nate Woodberry's Pulitzer prize–winning photos were legendary. Having her name associated with the images alone would be a coup for her career. This was getting better and better. "Can I see them?"

"Not yet," he said. "There's just one other thing that we need to be clear on." Setting his mug on the countertop, he moved closer to her and dipped his head so that they were face-to-face. "Are you listening?"

"Y-yes." She smelled the coffee on his breath and leaned in even closer, suddenly craving a secondhand jolt of caffeine. Her nipples tightened involuntarily, scraping against the inside of her sundress the way she hoped that his tongue one day would.

She hadn't been kidding when she'd suggested that they sleep together. She couldn't speak for him, but unless they jumped each other and got it out of the way, there was no way that she'd be able to fully concentrate on work.

For all his posturing, he wasn't completely unaffected, either. His Adam's apple bobbed not once but twice before he spoke and gave himself away. The idea that she could turn him on — that she *was* turning him on — caused the hair on the back of her neck to stand up in anticipation.

"When I take you to bed," he whispered into her open mouth, "sex between us will be anything but a nonissue. Got it?"

"Got it."

"Good." And then he kissed her.

CHAPTER 4

Already she was driving him crazy, Nate thought almost bitterly. They had been working together — and he was using the term *working* loosely — for a week now and he was just about at his wit's end. What was she doing that irritated the hell out of him? Nothing really, now that he was thinking about it, but then again, everything.

He was used to working alone, making his own schedule and following his own timetable, and having her underfoot all the time was seriously messing with his flow. He liked peace and quiet when he wasn't on location, time to gather his thoughts and decide how best to approach a situation, and she was a nonstop ball of chattering energy. He was territorial where his darkroom concerned, always had been, and she had somehow gotten into the habit of joining him there, touching everything and constantly hanging over his shoulder to see what he was doing, even though it was too dark to see a damn thing.

A couple of times he had thought about canceling their tentative partnership and banning her from coming within a hundred yards of him ever again. But she always managed to turn one of her dazzlingly coy smiles on him at exactly the right moment and make him lose his train of thought, let alone his resolve.

She was working her voodoo magic on the townspeople, too, which he guessed was a bonus. Just like every other recent town-hall meeting before it, last week's had turned into a small-scale riot, with Gwinnet County officials ultimately scurrying out a side door in order to avoid having to answer questions that they had no answers for. After they were gone, Tressie had kicked into high gear just in time to break up a fight between two men who had been best friends for over thirty years, and then she had somehow managed to get the men talking at length — right into the palm-size tape recorder that she'd brought along with her. By the time Nate and Tressie had excused themselves from the melee, she had conducted a handful of personal, one-on-one interviews with people who had been on the verge of violence just minutes before.

He had watched her work the room in impossibly high heels and a designer skirt suit that fit her like a second skin, and thought, *Tressie Valentine? Seriously?*

Growing up, he had never paid much attention to her, mainly because she'd been two years behind him in school and there had been plenty of girls his own age to keep him busy. And then when he had tracked her down in New York five years ago, he'd been too irate to focus on anything other than accomplishing his mission or to notice the details. And, of course, the Brazilian supermodel that he'd been tangled up with at the time had factored into the equation, too. She definitely hadn't done his attention span much good where anything and anyone else was concerned, either. What was her name? Monique? Jessica? Tangie? Damned if he could remember now, but the point was, Tressie hadn't even registered on his radar back then.

What he did remember about the supermodel was that she'd been sultry and seductive, and had eased into his consciousness slowly, engaging him degree by intriguing degree. And all the while he had been aware of her motives, quietly facilitating the means for her to get to him, and providing plenty of opportunities for the two of them to end up exactly where they'd been headed from the start — in bed. He had gone into their brief affair with his eyes wide-open and the rules clearly defined.

Not at all like what was going on between him and Tressie now. Nothing about her was the least bit subtle or sultry. Instead, everything about her was right *there,* in his face like an oncoming runaway train that he couldn't get away from. No mystery. No intrigue. No nothing. Just her, right *there.*

And suddenly he couldn't look away from her.

The kiss they'd shared hadn't been deep enough, long enough, wet enough to satisfy his curiosity. Not even close. He didn't know why he'd thought it would be. All it had done was make him thirsty for more of her and piss him off beyond belief. What kind of woman looked a man in the eyes and calmly suggested that they hop into bed together just to relieve the tension between them? A nutty, unstable, frighteningly bold one, he told himself and shook his head.

As if sensing the direction of his thoughts, she sighed softly and drew his eyes to her just in time to see her undo yet another button down the front of her sundress and pull her hair up off the back of her neck. The electric fan that she was sitting in front of was struggling under the heavy Georgia heat, and she was slowly wilting.

"It's like falling down a rabbit hole, isn't it?" he asked, pushing his chair back from the dining room table and stretching out his legs. They had been working at Tressie's place for the past three days, and the combination of the heat and the constant glow of his laptop's screen were starting to wear on his nerves. "Coming back to this place, I mean."

"A rabbit hole? Please." Tressie laughed, a light and cheerful sound that made him want to laugh, too. "Coming back here is like being in a time travel machine that's missing a few screws. I can't believe how old-fashioned it still is here. I mean, Atlanta is, what, an hour away? How can this place still be so behind the times? Who doesn't have central air-conditioning, for God's sake?"

"Miss Juanita was old-school." A picture of the woman in question formed in his mind and he smiled at it. She'd been his teacher in elementary school and then again in junior high, and he didn't recall ever seeing her smile in all that time. He did, however, recall being dragged by the scruff of his neck into her cloakroom for a paddling with embarrassing regularity. It made sense that she would maintain a home that was hotter than a sweatshop.

"So was Miss Merlene, but she had central air," Tressie came back. "And I don't care how small this town is, it should not take an hour and a half to deliver a pizza. God, I can't wait to get back to New York. The crime rate there is horrendous, the smog and pollution are awful, and the people aren't the nicest you'll ever meet. But at least you can get a decent latte." She slipped out of her chair at the other end of the rectangular table and disappeared into the kitchen. She returned a few seconds later with two bottles of cold water and tossed him one. Hers was already half-empty by the time she sat back down. "How in the world have you survived here for so long?"

"Easy," Nate said and drank deeply. "In the six months that I've been here, I've actually only *been* here for about a third of that time. And when I am here, I spend most of my time in my darkroom."

"Ma'Dear told me that you lived in Seattle."

"When I'm not on assignment, I do. But when my mother got sick, I started coming here more often to be with her. After she died, the eminent domain situation came up and I couldn't see myself just selling off her house and turning my back on the town. She probably would've haunted me for the rest of my life if I had."

Tressie's smile was lightning quick and teasing. "You always were a mama's boy."

"To the core and I refuse to be ashamed of it." He stood and walked the length of the table, coming to stand directly behind her chair. "I'll sell the house when the time is right. Maybe. What are you working on?"

"I'm almost done compiling a chronological history of Mercy, Georgia," she said as her fingers flew over the keyboard. "We know that the town was founded by freed slaves right after emancipation and that there was a white benefactor who sponsored the settlement. But I've only been able to go so far back before I start hitting dead ends. The original town charter mysteriously disappeared years and years ago, and no one seems to know the identity of the benefactor. Not that it matters much at this point, I guess, but still. It would be nice to know what the terms of the original charter were, wouldn't it?" She threw up her hands in defeat and let them fall noisily to her lap. "It's incredibly frustrating."

"I can imagine." From where he was standing, he had a perfect view down the front of her sundress and he didn't feel the slightest bit guilty about enjoying it. Incredibly frustrated — hell, yes — but guilty? No. He sucked in a deep breath and forced himself to look away. "You've been at it for too long," he decided suddenly. "Let's go out and get some fresh air, find something to eat. I'm half-starved." *And ready to pounce,* he thought as a smile lit up her face and shot a healthy dose of lust straight to his groin.

"Okay, but aren't you worried about people seeing the two of us together and jumping to conclusions?" Tressie teased. "You know how people here like to gossip." She fluffed out her hair as she stood, then straightened her sundress, dimpling up at him innocently the whole time.

If it hadn't been for the provocative neckline of her dress, her glossy red lips and the knowing gleam in her eyes, he thought as she flitted past him in search of her purse, she might've pulled the look off. And he might've saved himself from conceding a measure of personal defeat when he said matter-of-factly, "I'm more worried about what I might do to you if we stay cooped up in this house together for too much longer."

"Oh, well, then I guess we'd better get going." She slung her purse strap over her shoulder and gave him a look that clearly said, *Unless you've changed your mind and you want to . . .*

"Go," Nate barked with more force than he'd intended. Ushering her through the living room toward the door, he swung it open and stepped back so she could take the lead. "After you."

Okay, so maybe they were *both* nutty and unstable.

Two hours later, Nate reluctantly admitted to himself that there was no maybe about it. She was definitely unstable and so the hell was he. At least that's what he would tell the police when they came to arrest the two of them for trespassing on private property.

At after eleven o'clock on a weeknight, Moira Tobias had probably been asleep for hours, but that didn't mean that the household staff had also retired for the night. Any one of them could look out a window or wander outside for a breath of fresh air and spot them. There was also the possibility that Moira had installed a security system that no one knew about, in which case they had either already tripped it or were about to any second now. But neither scenario was compelling enough to stop him from hauling Tressie over the fence and racing her across the freshly mowed grass.

The tiny creek that was nestled in a hidden cove on Moira's property was far enough away from the main house that, once they found it, the chances of their being discovered were minimal. But as still and quiet as the night was, the chances of Tressie's cheerful, high-pitched voice carrying significantly increased the risk.

It was bad enough that she had come up with the bright idea to scale the privacy fence surrounding the rear perimeter of Moira's property and go for a midnight swim in the woman's creek, and even worse that he had allowed himself to be talked into going along with her harebrained plan. The last thing they needed was to be caught red-handed, wearing matching silly expressions and muttering lame excuses. Moira would probably have a heart attack, thinking that her home was about to be invaded by maniacs, and the rest of the town, once word got out, would have a field day with the gossip.

Tressie didn't seem concerned, though, and, watching her, Nate couldn't really say that he was, either. This wouldn't be the first time that he had sneaked onto Moira's property and gotten caught, so what the hell. Kicking off his leather sandals, he chose a spot in the grass near the creek bank, well away from the in-ground landscape lighting, and sat down to wait Tressie out.

She dipped her toes in first, testing the water temperature. Finding it cool, she gathered her sundress in her hands and waded into shallow water. When she was done squealing with delight because the water was chillier than she'd thought it would be, she glanced back at him over her shoulder.

"You coming in?" she called out, moving slowly toward the center of the creek where the water was deeper. Slowly, it rose to her thighs, and so did her dress.

"You go in much farther and that dress is going to be in trouble," he said, secretly wishing that she would take pity on him and take it off. Being so close to her this past week and having to look but not touch had been hell on him. The least she could do for a dying man was put him out of his misery.

"So will my panties," she quipped. "But then again, they've been wet pretty much since I saw you again, so it really doesn't matter. Does it?"

Or not, he thought as he sucked in a sharp breath. Just like that, he was hard as a rock. "You shouldn't say things like that."

"Why? Because you don't want to hear it?"

"No," he said, rolling up from the grass and pulling his T-shirt over his head as he stood. "Because it makes me hard." To prove his point, he unsnapped his jeans and stepped out of both the constricting denim and his underwear at the same time. Suddenly free, his penis tightened, expanded and then bobbed in the night air impatiently.

As hot as he suddenly was, Nate barely felt the chilly water when he waded into the creek. He kept his eyes on hers and watched them grow wider and wider with every step that he took in her direction. "I told myself that we wouldn't do this," he said, walking slowly. "I can think of a million reasons why we shouldn't."

"We can't stand each other," Tressie put in helpfully, and he smiled.

"There's that. Plus, you're not my type." He thought about it for a second, visualized himself sliding inside her and swallowed the lump in his throat. He was and always had been a sexual man, and he'd been with his share of women in his adult years. But right now he couldn't think of a woman in his past, present or future that he'd ever wanted more than he wanted Tressie. What the hell was she doing to him? "You shouldn't be, anyway."

"But?"

"But I still want you." Close enough to reach out and touch her, he searched her eyes. "What is this? What are we doing?"

Now it was Tressie's turn to smile. "Calling a truce." She took a moment to slip her dress over her head and toss it up on the creek bank. The moment her heavy breasts bounced free, her nipples puckered and his mouth watered.

"Jesus, your breasts are beautiful." Unable to stop himself, he reached out and smoothed the pad of his thumb across a swollen nipple. She shuddered and it was all he could do to keep from scooping her up by her round, juicy ass cheeks and sitting her down on him. Soon, he promised himself. Soon.

As if she were reading his mind, Tressie smiled a secret smile as she closed the distance between them, stood on the tip of her toes and flicked her tongue across his nipple. She moaned when it hardened instantly and moved in to enjoy the other one, but he stopped her with a hand on her arm.

"No, sugar," he whispered, "it's my turn now."

■ ■ ■ ■

What happened next almost blew Tressie's mind.

She forgot to breathe when Nate grabbed her by the shoulders and pulled her into him.

She flattened her hands against his chest to steady herself as her head rocked back and a long, kittenish meow worked its way up her throat and out her mouth.

Her next breath was sucked into Nate's mouth, along with her tongue, and from that moment on she was lost. The kiss was wild and urgent, wet because their mouths were wide-open and fused together hungrily, the most erotic moment that Tressie had ever experienced. She didn't think it was possible for her nipples to get any harder, but they did. She didn't think it was possible for her inner walls to get any slicker with honey, but they did. She was practically dripping by the time he fisted a hand in her hair and broke the kiss.

A sharp cry shot out of her mouth when he tugged on her hair and moved her head even farther back, exposing her neck. Like a vampire, his mouth fastened onto the skin there and feasted. His lips glided, his teeth nipped and his tongue stroked, and she heard herself making noises of delight that she had never heard before. Loud, unintelligible sounds that she didn't know she was capable of making.

"Shhh," Nate whispered in her ear. Then his hands began gliding over her skin and his mouth got busy again, and the warning slipped right out of her head. She tried to touch him the way he was touching her, but she was almost limp with excitement. The best she could do was brace herself and hope the water didn't carry her off.

He palmed her butt and squeezed, separated her buttocks and kneaded expertly, then slipped a finger inside her from behind and destroyed her. "Oh, God," she choked out just before an orgasm rolled through her body from head to toe and buckled her knees. Her inner walls spasmed, craving something hard and solid to grip, and her honey flowed hot and thick. She reached between them and wrapped a hand around his length, squeezing gently and sighing wistfully when his hips surged forward and a low growl lit the air.

Swearing viciously, Nate banded an arm around Tressie's waist and lifted her out of the water. Her breasts bounced and swayed in the air in front of his face for all of two seconds before his mouth captured a nipple and began sucking it greedily. He was still sucking when he laid her on her back in the grass and braced himself over her. His mouth roamed from one breast to the other, licking and nipping Tressie into a frenzy. This time, the sensations were so intense that she couldn't have made a sound if her life depended on it. Her mouth was frozen into a delighted O of pleasure as his tongue drew patterns on her skin. The fingers on one hand lost themselves in his mane of silky hair, while her other hand cupped her breasts and fed them to him eagerly.

"I don't have anything with me," Nate tore his mouth away from her breast long enough to hiss. His expression was mixture of regret and tenuously banked passion. "Dammit."

Dammit was right. But Tressie wasn't quite ready to put out the fire that had started between them just yet. Once again, her hand found his jutting erection and squeezed, coaxing a strangled moan from his throat.

"Tressie . . ."

"Lie down," she told him and helped him do just that with a gentle push to his chest. When he was right where she wanted him, lying back in the grass with his hair fanned out around his face and shoulders, she slanted her body across his and tried, very nearly with success, to swallow his penis whole. He was long and thick, and she was something of a neophyte, but what she lacked in skill she more than made up for in intensity.

A shocked, hoarse, feral cry shot out of his mouth and, encouraged, Tressie's head began moving up and down his length. His hips rotated in time to her ministrations, slowly at first, and then picking up speed. Soon he was pumping into her mouth wantonly, moaning erratically and threading his fingers through her hair. The sounds he made urged Tressie on, until she was moaning herself, on the verge of another bone-melting orgasm.

As if he was reading her mind, Nate slipped a hand between her thighs and homed in on her nub. The second he pressed the pad of his finger against the slick, rigid bud, Tressie's body jerked as if she'd been hit with a live wire. Her mouth popped off Nate's straining flesh and she threw her head back to sing a long, shaky, a cappella note to the sky. Her impending orgasm sent electric vibrations through her body, stealing her breath and lulling her into a sense of euphoria. She was so caught up in the feelings overtaking her that she didn't physically register Nate's intentions until she felt his warm hands palming her butt and she felt herself being lifted into the air. A few seconds later, he was settling her on top of him so that she could take his length deeper into her mouth and he could introduce his mouth to her most intimate place.

"Oh, God," Tressie panted. Was she coming again? It wasn't possible, was it? Nate's tongue uncurled between her nether lips, and the answer to her questions keened out of her mouth in one long wail. "Yessssss."

She opened up for his tongue like a flower, and his eyes slid closed on a shuddering breath. Her honey was sweet to the taste, like a Georgia peach, and just as juicy. *Addictive,* he thought as he gripped her ass and tongue-kissed her most sensitive spot mercilessly. He lapped at it, sucked it out of its hiding place and flicked the tip of his tongue back and forth, around and around, until she was riding his mouth with urgent thrusts. When he sensed that she was about to come again, he withdrew from her hot button and let his tongue dance up and down the length of her slick divide.

Her mouth was still latched on to him, matching his rhythm stroke for stroke, and pushing him closer and closer to the edge. He had held back for as long as he could, but with those soft, silky lips sliding up and down his shaft, rhythmically tightening on the head and sucking his soul out of him with lightning speed, he was fighting a losing battle.

His tongue sought out her button just as her thighs starting shaking and her breathless pants became high-pitched moans. His grip on her ass tightened when she tried to escape his lapping tongue, and his strokes, long and deep, quickened until he swore he could feel the back of her throat. He released his hold on her just long enough to slip a trembling hand between them and take control of his pulsing penis, snatching it from the tight suction of her lips mere seconds before he came like a geyser. Then he gripped her again and buried his face in her slippery folds while she rode out a seemingly endless spasm.

Neither of them moved for several seconds, and then Tressie slid off him and stretched out in the grass next to him. He would've been content to lie there for a little while longer, at least until he caught his breath, but it wasn't to be.

"Last one in the creek is a rotten egg," Tressie said, jumping to her feet and taking off down the creek bank toward the water.

"You've got to be kidding me." One eye opened just in time to see Tressie hit the water with a loud splash and disappear underneath its surface. She resurfaced on the far side of the creek and slicked her dripping hair back from her face, smiling from ear to ear. He stared at her for several seconds and then released the breath that he hadn't realized he'd been holding.

It's just a summer fling, he told himself as he got to his feet and strolled toward the water. *A mutually satisfying summer fling.*

So why was he reaching for her as soon as she was close enough to touch, craving yet another taste of her even though her taste was still on his tongue?

"Come here, sugar," he said, though the command was unnecessary because she had already waded into the circle of his arms. "Put your tongue in my mouth." She did and he began to suck on it.

Then it all came to a screeching halt.

"Who's out there?" a voice called out.

Tressie reared back, looking around wildly. "Uh-oh," she croaked and took off running.

CHAPTER 5

Tressie was in the lead, stomping through the water loudly and splashing it in every direction as she scrambled for the creek bank. She heard Nate behind her and felt his hands at her waist, urging her out of the water.

"Where's my dress?" she asked as she wrestled with the dress in question, trying to wriggle it up and over hips. Instead of sliding on smoothly, it clung to her wet skin and irritated the hell out of her. The fact that she'd slung her purse around her neck first and now it was dangling in front of her and getting in the way wasn't helping. Cursing under her breath, she twirled the thing around her neck to her back like a hula hoop.

"You're putting it on," Nate hissed, yanking his shorts on. He stuffed his underwear in one pocket and their flashlight in another, and he snatched her panties up from the grass. "Here," he said, tossing the lacy pink bundle at her. She caught it on the fly and then snatched up her sandals. Shoes in hand and T-shirt half on and half off, he checked the perimeter of the creek and then motioned silently for her to head for the fence.

"Who's out there?" the voice called out again.

A flashlight clicked on in the distance, behind a small stand of trees, and Tressie dropped into a crouching position. "Let's go!" She looked around frantically for Nate and finally spotted him several feet ahead of her, almost at the fence. "Nate! Wait up!"

"I said 'let's go' two minutes ago!" At the fence, he took a second to bend down and put on his sandals while Tressie raced toward him.

The flashlight's beam was getting closer, and Tressie's heart was pounding. She ran faster than she ever had in her life and that was saying something, because she'd been the star of the Mercy High School track team about a million years ago. She was pretty sure that she'd dropped her panties in the grass a few feet back, but there was no way she was going back for them, even if they were her favorite pair. Nate had already scaled the fence and was straddling the top, ready to grab her and haul her up and over, if only she could get there already.

"Is anybody out there?"

There was the voice again and it was getting closer, along with that damned flashlight beam. It was probably just one of Moira's ancient house staff, come outside to see what all the noise down by the creek was about, but still. This wasn't exactly the way that she'd planned to make Moira's acquaintance again after all these years, with her panties on the ground at the woman's feet, grass in her hair and one of her breasts dangerously close to spilling out of her dress.

"Wait up!" she hissed at Nate again.

"Hurry up, Tressie!"

The grass was steady and dry underneath her feet and she was making good time. A few more feet and she'd be up and over the fence in no time. Getting ready for the jump, she reached up for Nate's hands at the same time that the ground shifted underneath her. Too shocked to utter a sound, she wobbled sideways and lost her footing. When her ankle twisted, pain shot up her calf and she would've screamed if the ground hadn't chosen that exact moment to disappear. With a comical "Oh" lingering in the air in her wake, the ground opened up and swallowed her.

"Tressie!"

Her shoes flew in opposite directions as she landed on her butt on what she guessed was hardpacked dirt and sat there for a moment, getting her bearings. She heard Nate's voice above her and got to her feet. She rotated her ankle and breathed a sigh a relief when it didn't seem to be seriously injured. The top of the hole that she'd fallen down into was a few feet over her head, far enough away that she couldn't reach it, but close enough that she could see up and out of it, to the night sky above. Thank God she hadn't done herself any real harm. Other than her butt being a little sore and her ankle complaining slightly, she was fine. Her purse was still behind her, dangling from her neck and slapping against her back.

The landscaping lights up above were no help to her down here, but at least she could clearly see the opening that had swallowed her. She stood directly underneath it. "Down here," she called back. "I think I fell down a rabbit hole. Toss me the flashlight."

Instead of the flashlight, Nate's legs appeared in the hole. Slowly, he lowered himself down into the ground. Tressie moved back to make room for him, laughing when he landed on his feet like a super-size cat. "Great," she said when he was finally down there with her, "now we're both trapped."

"I've been in worse hiding places than this — trust me," Nate murmured, looking around in the darkness. "We'll give it a few minutes and see if whoever is up there leaves, and then we'll climb back out and get the hell out of here. Remind me to strangle you for getting us in this mess sometime tomorrow, would you?"

"Is anybody out here?" the voice said from almost directly above them.

"Shhh," Nate whispered, moving away from the opening and taking Tressie with him. He pressed her back against a cool dirt wall and held her there with his body against hers. "Don't make a sound," he whispered in her ear.

"Hello?" the voice above called.

"Do you think they know about this hole?" Tressie wanted to know.

"They will if you keep talking. Shhh."

She slapped the hand that he placed over her mouth away. "What if there are snakes down here or . . . or rats?"

"Would you please stop it?" he breathed close to her face.

"No, I will not stop," she whispered back. "There could be a ten-foot-long snake somewhere down here right now, waiting to swallow me whole, and those things don't even have teeth. How is that going to work?"

"If you're out here somewhere," the voice above them called out, "I have your panties. You'd better come out and get them, because they sure ain't my size." A few seconds of silence passed and then, "Sure wish they was, though. Cute."

Tressie's head fell back against the dirt wall. "Oh, my God." It took her a few seconds to realize that Nate was silently cracking up. His body was vibrating against hers softly, in an effort, she guessed, to keep quiet. She pushed at his chest, and he stumbled a few steps back. "You think this is funny?"

"Hell, yes," he managed to say between chuckles. "Don't you?"

"No." She was incredulous. "Those were my favorite panties!" That only made him laugh harder. Up above them, the voice was still talking but, thankfully, it sounded farther away.

"Probably some kids out here fooling around," it said thoughtfully. "I told Miss Moira that she needs to get some guard dogs. Ain't no telling how many babies been made out here by this creek."

They waited a few minutes to be sure that the coast was clear, then Nate switched on the flashlight, shining it directly in her face. "Are you all right? Let me see your ankle."

"Get that thing out of my face," Tressie snapped, throwing up her hands to shield her face from the surprisingly high-powered beam. "My ankle is fine — just a little sore." She reached for him and then slipped behind him. She grabbed fistfuls of his T-shirt, pressed up against him and peeked out from behind his shoulder. "Look around and see what else is hiding down here with us." Dreading what the flashlight might reveal, she squeezed her eyes shut and held her breath, waiting.

When Nate went completely still, she feared the worst.

"What is it? What do you see?"

He said nothing and, after several seconds of intense silence, Tressie opened one eye and then the other, leaning sideways slightly to see around him. "What is it?"

"Do you see what I see?" Nate finally asked.

"Y-yes," she squeaked out, staring. Her mouth eventually fell open. "Oh, my God."

"You keep saying that."

"I know, but I mean it this time." She stepped out from behind him and crept around the space in her bare feet. One thing in particular caught her attention and held it. She reached for it tentatively, as if it might suddenly strike out at her. "Look —"

"Don't touch anything," Nate barked just before she would've touched the object of her attention. "Come back over here to me, sugar. We can't disturb anything." He held out a hand to her and she took it, vaguely registering the fact that her hand fit perfectly in his. "Come on, sugar. Watch your step."

Back in Nate's arms, Tressie let the sob that had been building in her chest escape. After the first one, a floodgate seemed to open and she was sobbing uncontrollably. Suddenly the air around them seemed cooler and somehow . . . sad, and she shivered. The space was no bigger than a small bedroom. The walls, floors and ceiling were made of packed dirt with wooden slats visible in some places. Along the back wall, crude drawings had been etched deep into the dirt, but time had obscured their clarity.

Still, Tressie knew. She *knew*. And in case she didn't, there could be no mistaking the archaic and rusted artifacts scattered on the floor in a dark corner. She had reached for the least of them, a bowl, and she would've picked it up and marveled at it, held it in the palms of her hands, if Nate hadn't had the presence of mind to stop her. Her fingers itched to touch . . . feel . . . experience, but he was right. They couldn't disturb the sanctity of this space, not yet.

"Your camera," she said, frantically wiping the tears from her eyes. "You have to bring your camera here. You have to —"

"I know," he cut in almost reverently. His grip on her waist tightened and she heard him swallow. "But first, sugar, let's just stand here for a minute and feel this place." He pressed a kiss to the top of her head and then her forehead, and she felt her heart shift in her chest a little bit. "Let's just let it feel us."

"Do you know what this is, Nate?" Of course he did, but she couldn't help asking the question anyway. This was too big, too important not to speak aloud into the universe. "Do you know what we just found? What this means?"

"Sure I do, sugar. It means you didn't just fall down a rabbit hole. You discovered a stop on the Underground Railroad."

They were both riding high on the impact of the discovery that they had made less than an hour ago, and neither of them was thinking straight. But then, neither of them really wanted to be. There were calls to make, people to talk to and strategies to plan, but none of it mattered right now.

First, there was this, Nate thought as he rolled a magnum-size condom onto his stiff and aching penis and lay back in the middle of his bed. A rumbling purr started in the center of his chest and crawled up his throat, slowly curling out of his mouth as Tressie slid on top of him. Her breasts bounced and jiggled in front of his face for all of five seconds before his mouth opened, his tongue shot out and his lips closed over a plump nipple. He sucked it deep inside his mouth and listened to her meow like a kitten.

First, there was this, he thought again. The rest could wait.

Down below, she gripped him and slid her slick divide up and down his length, gasping for air every time the head of his penis pushed up and across her engorged clitoris. He wondered through the fog rapidly clouding his brain if she knew how each of the little ecstatic sounds she made landed against his eardrums, if she had any idea how close he was to exploding because of them.

Unable to stop himself, Nate reached down between them and swept Tressie's hands out and away from their bodies. He threaded his fingers through hers and held them on the mattress on either side of his head as his hips rotated between her thighs. When his length was up against her sopping-wet opening, he entered her with one long, deep thrust.

"Ahhh," Tressie threw her head back and cried out. "Ahhh," she cried again when his hips rotated quickly, causing him to withdraw almost completely and surge up into her again.

"Damn," Nate hissed with her breast still in his mouth. Feeling like a wild, untamed animal, he rolled over and reversed their positions. Tressie's legs instinctively opened as wide as possible and bowed back, and his eyes slid closed on a low moan. Bracing himself on his hands over her, he gritted his teeth and buried himself in her scorching heat to the hilt. She was almost unbearably tight and hot, and dripping wet and silky and . . .

He lost his mind inside her and his hips took on a life of their own, pumping and rolling to their own rhythm. The bed shook beneath them and, underneath him, Tressie's body vibrated violently. Her head was thrown back, her eyes squeezed shut and her mouth opened, but no sound emerged. His strokes rendered her silent, unable to do anything except squeeze her bouncing breasts in her hands and take what he was giving her.

He was the one shouting as if he had suddenly taken leave of his senses. Growling like a beast and sucking in deep gulps of air to keep himself from passing out. God, she was exquisite and she felt so damn good that he couldn't stop himself from pushing and pushing and pushing inside her.

"Ah, yes, sugar," he crooned when Tressie's legs bowed back even farther and her knees damn near met her ears. "That's right. Open up for me. Give this to me . . . all of it."

She did open up and then her walls clamped shut around him, closing him into a velvet fist that he wanted to stay trapped inside of forever. A gentle thumping at the base of his spine alerted him to the fact that forever wasn't meant to be, though. He lost his breath and before he could catch it again, he was coming, shouting her name and issuing some kind of ancient tribal-sounding call, all at the same time.

While he was still sprawled on top of her, searching for his breath and not finding it, she turned her head, slipped her tongue inside his mouth like a dream and found his. All tongue and teeth, the kiss seemed to go on and on, until she finally ended it with a soft, lingering peck.

Ignoring his protesting groan, she pushed her fingers up into the depths of his hair, cupped his still-tingling scalp and gently urged his head down onto the pillow next to hers.

His last coherent thought, before he fell asleep lying on top of her and still buried inside her, was, *Tressie Valentine? Seriously?*

"Hello?"

"Miss Valentine, this is Norman Harper."

"Uh . . . just a second, please."

Mentally kicking herself for not taking time to look at the caller-ID screen before answering, Tressie tucked her cell phone between her head and shoulder, and glanced back over her shoulder nervously. Nate was still asleep and snoring lightly, thank God. She climbed out of bed as quietly as possible and grabbed her sundress off the lampshade on her way out of the bedroom. She went into the bathroom off the hallway and closed the door behind her.

"Good morning, Mr. Harper," she half whispered into the phone, automatically shifting into professional mode. "What can I do for you?"

"I think a better question would be, what can I do for you, Miss Valentine," he said. "Have you thought any more about the offer that Consolidated Investments made you? We would really like to take possession of your house as soon as possible. I assume you're still interested in selling?"

"Um, yes, I am, but there are still a few minor details that I need to take care of," Tressie lied. Nate had helped her finish packing up and clearing out the house days ago. Most of the furniture was safely in storage, and there was a slightly shabby but clean local motel that she could check in to anytime she wanted. But she wasn't quite ready to turn over Ma'Dear's house to Consolidated Investments, even if she did desperately need the money that the sale would bring her. Nate had made his opinion of what she had come to Mercy to do very clear in the days since they had agreed to work together and, for some reason, his opinion mattered.

He's not your husband, Tressie, a little voice in the back of her mind insisted. *Who cares what he thinks? Think of Vanessa Valentino and what this money could do for her, for her career. You want your career back, don't you?*

"Can you give me a little more time?" she heard herself ask. "A few more days, maybe?"

"Sure," Norman said easily, "but I'm sure

you're aware of the time-sensitive nature of our offer. We pride ourselves on being a fair-minded company, which is why we've been very generous in our offers to purchase certain homes in Mercy. I hope I don't have to remind you, Miss Valentine, that once the eminent domain laws go into effect, those offers will decrease significantly, and some may even be rescinded."

"No, you don't, Mr. Harper. I'm well aware of how eminent domain laws work. But I do need a few more days to get my affairs in order. Would it be possible for you to email me the documents? That way I can familiarize myself with everything before I call you back on, say, Tuesday?"

"Tuesday sounds good, Miss Valentine. I'll have my assistant send you digital copies of the purchase offer for your review and look forward to your call."

"Tuesday." She hung up and jumped into her sundress quickly. What the hell was she going to do when Tuesday rolled around and she still wasn't sure whether or not she wanted to sign on the dotted line?

Don't think about it right now, Tressie.

Right. That sounded like a plan. A good one, too. Between now and Tuesday, she had plenty of stuff to do to keep her occupied. There was the final draft of her write-up on

Mercy's history to get through, Nate's photo journal to help put together and a publicity plan to come up with. Norman Harper and Consolidated Investments could wait a few more days. By then, she'd have a clearer idea of what direction she definitely needed to go in — sell the house and land and make out like a bandit with the money from the sale, or make out like a bandit from the publicity and credibility that her work with Nate would bring her. The only thing she was sure about right now was that she couldn't have it both ways.

Okay, Tressie. Think.

A lengthy, heartwarming spread in major newspapers across the country was good, but was it good enough? A few sound bites during television news broadcasts would be very beneficial, but would they be enough?

Maybe, maybe not, she thought as she paced the floor in the bathroom. When it came to the common man going up against powerful corporate entities, the outcome was always a crapshoot. Anything could happen. And, sadly, she hadn't heard of very many instances when the common man had prevailed. Unless she and Nate came up with a bulletproof plan of action, Mercy was going down, heartwarming story or not.

She thought about the discovery that she

and Nate had made last night. Stumbling upon an authentic stop on the Underground Railroad was big news, but what did it really mean? And if there was one stop, what were the chances that there were more undiscovered stops around town somewhere? Could they find others? And even if they did find other stops in town, what would stop big business from simply erecting signs acknowledging their locations and tearing down and building around them?

She sank down onto the toilet seat and put her head in her hands, thinking. What they needed to do was make a big splash somehow. But that was easier said than done in a place like Mercy, Georgia. The biggest claim to fame that the place had going for it was the fact that Pamela Mayes had once lived in the town's struggling little children's home. . . .

And Pamela Mayes was the last person she could expect to help her in any way. But maybe, just maybe, Pam would help Nate.

Tressie was still working out how she was going to pull off whatever it was that she was going to pull off when she crept back into the bedroom and climbed back into bed.

CHAPTER 6

Nate called his publicist first and instructed her to make contact with the Anthropology Department at the University of Atlanta. While he waited for Julia to call him back, he put in some calls to a few journalist friends of his that owed him favors. Even without their newest discovery to factor in, it was time to start creating a buzz about the situation in Mercy, Georgia. If Julia lived up to her reputation, and she always did, people in high places would be talking about what was going on in Mercy long before the story hit the news circuit, but it wouldn't hurt for him to do an interview or two in the meantime.

Julia called him back an hour later with good news. The university was sending out an anthropological crew to survey the site first thing in the morning. They would be prepared to begin excavation as early as tomorrow afternoon if the site was found to be authentic. Sure that it would be, he disconnected the call and dialed Moira Tobias's number next. He figured the least he could do was alert her beforehand that her property was about to be the object of national attention.

Smiling at what he knew would be Moira's reaction, he packed up his camera equipment while he listened to her phone ring and waited for her to pick up. He looked up when the shower in his bathroom shut off and a dripping-wet, gloriously naked Tressie stepped out onto a bath mat. Tracking every move she made like a hunter on the prowl, he almost forgot that he was on the phone until Moira's genteel Southern voice snapped him out of his brief trancelike state.

"Hello?"

He had to swallow before speaking to wet his dry throat. "Moira, this is Nate Woodberry," he said into the phone. "How are you?"

Whatever Moira's response was, it was lost in translation. She could've been speaking in French, for all Nate heard and understood. He must've been speaking in French, too, because he heard himself responding to her, carrying on a conversation, but really had no idea what they were actually talking about. Something about a late-afternoon visit. She would have her cook prepare lunch for them and they could eat out on the back sun porch. Like old times, she said, and sounded excited.

He murmured something about looking forward to seeing her and stifled an impatient sigh when she launched into a long-winded recollection of the last time he had visited with her, which had been shortly after his mother's funeral. Finally, she remembered that she had been out in the south garden when the phone had rung and needed to get back to her prize-winning roses before the heat overwhelmed them. Ending the call with a hurried pleasantry, he dropped his cell and camera case on the bed, then strolled into the bathroom with one thing and one thing only on his mind.

"Here, sugar, let me help you with that," he said, taking the towel that Tressie was using to dry herself off and picking up where she left off.

Seeing the hooded look in his eyes, she blushed and grinned knowingly. "Don't get any ideas," she warned as he crouched down in front of her and smoothed the towel down the length of one toned leg. "I still have to go home and change, and if I heard correctly, you have a date with Moira Tobias."

"This won't take long," he promised, and pointed his tongue in the direction of the lovely, clean-shaven treasure between her thighs.

Moira Tobias was still out on the south lawn, piddling in her rose garden, when he arrived for their lunch date hours later. He spotted her in the distance as he drove up to the main house and decided to bypass ringing the bell and go directly to her. He parked his Navigator along the circular driveway and used the massive wraparound porch to segue to the rolling lawn behind it.

She wore a wide-brimmed straw hat as a defense against the sun's bright rays, so she didn't see him approaching until he was within a few feet of where she was kneeling in the dirt and his shadow fell across her. She looked up and broke into a wide smile.

"Nathaniel, how nice to see you!" She took the hand he extended and got to her feet slowly, brushing dirt from the knees of her gardening slacks daintily. "I'm so glad you called. Last I spoke to Pamela, she mentioned that you were on assignment someplace in Africa. I worried for you, being so far away, doing God knows what." She lifted her cheek for the kiss he dropped there and purred with maternal satisfaction.

"It's a relief to know that I can stop worrying, at least for a little while, anyway. Where will you go off to next?"

"I haven't decided," Nate replied, smiling down at the tiny woman. She had always been petite, but in her old age she seemed to get even smaller and more delicate every time he saw her. The perpetual sparkle in her bright green eyes was still there, though, despite the fact that her flaming-red hair had long since gone completely white and age spots covered the backs of her graceful hands. "I plan to hang around town for the next little while — see how things here go before I leave again." When she was ready, he wrapped an arm around her waist and walked with her across the lawn toward the house.

"Ah, things here," she said thoughtfully. "It's quite a mess, isn't it? All this town charter business and people quarreling nonstop. It's never been like this before. I've lived in this house all my life. I was born here and before that my ancestors were born here, and now the state tells me that I may lose it. It worries me constantly."

"You and everyone else in town. A lot of people will lose the only home they've ever known if the state doesn't do right by them."

"Where will we go?"

120

"Hopefully, it won't come to that," Nate said as they approached the back porch.

"We need a miracle."

On cue, a maid stepped out onto the porch to greet them. "Miss Moira, lunch is ready to be served whenever you're ready." The elderly black woman's eyes landed on Nate and an easy smile curved her lips. "Well, if it isn't the great Nathaniel Woodberry. Didn't I read an article of yours just last month in *Time* magazine?"

"*National Geographic,*" Nate said, chuckling. "It's good to see you, Janice."

"You, too. Are you staying for lunch?"

"Of course he is," Moira cut in, waving an impatient hand. She climbed the steps slowly, with Nate's hand at her back and Janice's hand at her elbow. "You don't think I'm going to eat that entire Black Forest cake that you baked all by myself, do you?"

"It's been known to happen," Janice murmured, and winked at Nate. "Come along, Miss Moira. I'll help you freshen up. Nate, you make yourself comfortable, and I'll bring you a nice glass of iced tea in just a second."

"Make it a cold beer and you've got a deal."

After the women had disappeared inside the house, Nate sank into a cushioned chair at the patio table on the far end of the porch. From where he was sitting, only the path leading down to the creek was visible. From the second or third floor, though, the creek was probably easy to spot. He wondered which one of Moira's house staff had almost caught him and Tressie the other night. It would be interesting to learn the fate of her favorite pink-lace panties.

Janice sailed out onto the porch, carrying a tray of drinks. She set the tray down on the table, handed him an ice-cold beer and stood back with her hands on her hips, considering him. "So what's this I hear about you keeping time with Juanita Valentine's granddaughter?" she blurted out without a hint of finesse.

"Well, now, sugar, there's keeping time and then there's keeping time," Nate said carefully before tipping the frosty bottle up to his mouth and taking a sip. "Sort of like the way you keep time with Jessie Hawkins on Friday nights, when everybody knows you also keep time with Kenny Fisher Monday through Thursday. Wouldn't you agree?"

Caught, Janice stared at Nate for several seconds through narrowed eyes. Then she noticed the teasing gleam in his eyes and burst out laughing. "I guess that's a nice

122

way of telling me to mind my own business," she said, waving a hand at him. Still laughing, she poured a glass of iced tea for Moira and set it on the table near the empty chair across from him. "I guess I better, too. Let me go and see what's taking Miss Moira so long. Lunch will be cold by the time she gets ready to eat."

Moira stepped out onto the porch just then. She had changed into fresh summer slacks and a matching top, and had secured her hair at the nape of her neck with a jeweled barrette. "Ah, Janice, here you are. I was wondering if one of the many ghosts that are always haunting the main house was in charge of watching the pots you left boiling on the stove. None of them spoke up when I passed through the kitchen, so I think you'd better go in and see what's going on."

Janice rolled her eyes on her way back inside, leaving Moira and Nate chuckling quietly in her wake. After the door closed behind her, Moira turned to Nate and unleashed a dazzling and uncomfortably familiar smile on him. "So . . . tell me. What's this I hear about you keeping time with Tressie Valentine?"

He was still tap-dancing around the question when Janice served lunch fifteen minutes later. Moira seemed to be enjoying his inability to provide a clear answer and didn't let him off the hook until she had spread a linen napkin over her lap and picked up her fork. "You haven't changed a bit, Nathaniel. You're still as cagey and evasive as you were as a boy. I think that's what Pamela always loved most about you. You wouldn't be her conscience —" His eyebrows shot up in surprise and she giggled demurely. "How could you be when you were always her partner in crime? But you were the keeper of her secrets. She trusted you then just as much as she trusts you now. I always envied your relationship."

"The two of you have a special bond," he reminded her, and cut into his own steak. Here was a minefield of past hurts, recriminations and complex emotions. And he no more wanted to get into it with her than the look on her face said that she did. Five years was a long time, but sometimes it wasn't long enough. "Have you spoken with Pam lately?"

"Just yesterday." Moira was clearly relieved at the change in direction. "She called to check on me, but of course I ended up asking all the questions and doing most of the talking. She's in, I believe she said, San Francisco, on tour. Oh, and Nikki emails me all the time. I can't believe she's already graduated from college and is ready to strike out on her own." Nikki was Pam's daughter. "Next, I'll be receiving a wedding invitation, and then I'll know that I've truly gotten old. Chad Junior is, what, four now?"

"Almost five."

"Such a beautiful boy," Moira mused wistfully. As if the thought had just occurred to her, she straightened in her chair and narrowed her eyes on Nate's face. "Why didn't you ever marry and have children, Nate?"

"No time, I guess." He shrugged nonchalantly, as if he had never asked himself the very same question. "At this point, Pam's kids are probably the closest I'll ever get to having my own and I'm fine with that." It was on the tip of his tongue to turn the question around on her, but he caught himself before he could put his foot in his mouth. "They're enough."

"If you say so."

For the next few minutes, they ate in silence. Then Janice stuck her head out the door.

"Are you ready for dessert, Miss Moira? Nate?"

Moira deferred to Nate. "Should we have some dessert?"

"If you say so," he came back, and made

her laugh.

While Janice cleared their lunch dishes and set out heaping slices of Black Forest cake, Nate's eyes scanned the massive lawn, barely registering the stables and the artfully landscaped gardens. He zeroed in on the path leading to the creek and decided that it was time to bring up the reason for his visit. He waited until Janice had returned to the house before speaking.

"Which one of your staff found a pair of ladies' panties down by the creek the other night, Moira?"

Her green eyes lit up with humor. "Um . . . Harriet, I believe. You wouldn't happen to know who they belong to, would you?" She looked as though she wanted to say more but didn't.

"Of course not," he lied smoothly. "But I will admit to being on your property that night, down at the creek. I found something very interesting down there, Moira, and I'm wondering if you even know it's there."

"Oh, you mean the Underground Railroad stop? Certainly, I'm aware that it's there, Nate. My grandparents were abolitionists and so were my great-grandparents." She set her fork down slowly and wiped her mouth, staring at him. "It's been years since I've been out there to see it for myself, but

I do find myself going down to the wine cellar quite often in my old age."

"The wine cellar?"

"Yes. There used to be an underground tunnel, leading from the wine cellar to the tunnel and vice versa. When runaway slaves were brought here, they were hidden in the underground space you found out there. From there, they were led into the house through the tunnel and hidden in a small room behind the cellar. The tunnel was closed off during the Civil War, I believe." Pushing back from the table and getting to her feet, Moira held out a hand to him. "Would you like to see the wine cellar, Nate?"

He was out of his seat before she finished posing the question. "I would love to."

In the dark, dusty wine cellar, as he stood at the doorway of the secret room in the rear of the cellar and breathed in the aura of the small space, he told Moira about his plans for the Underground Railroad stops on her property and for the town. He wasn't completely surprised when she agreed to have an archaeological team invade her private space, but he breathed a heavy sigh of relief just the same.

"Moira, you're a gem," he told her, kissing her hand gently. She blushed prettily and, again, there was the smile that he knew all too well on her lips. "How can I ever repay you?"

"You'll feature me in the story you write, of course." She smoothed a hand down the front of her blouse and then fluffed her hair. "And you'll get a few pictures of me, too, won't you? You did bring your camera with you, didn't you?"

Tressie was in awe.

She had seen Nate's work plenty of times, in magazines and newspapers, and once on display at a showing at an art gallery in SoHo. But there was nothing like being about to touch the prints he created, to handle them delicately just minutes after they had been deemed dry enough and ready for human consumption. And consume them she did.

One after another, she held up the prints, turned them this way and that way, peering at them from all different angles, up close and then at arm's length, seeing something different each time she looked at the same print.

"These are gorgeous," she whispered. He had taken numerous shots of both the underground hiding space and the secret room behind Moira's wine cellar, and something about them demanded quiet reverence. The solemn mood of the black-and-white shots sent chills up and down her spine. The vibrancy of the color shots made her heart rate spike excitedly. She couldn't stop staring at them. "Oh, my God, Nate. Look what you did. These are . . . so powerful that they're heartbreaking." Hands trembling slightly, she set the stack of photos down on the countertop in his darkroom and turned to face him. "Which ones are we using in the story?"

"I can't decide," he said, uncrossing his ankles and coming away from the cabinet, which he had been leaning back against, and across the room. He crossed the room with lazy strides, reminding her that he had been awake through the night working in his darkroom while she had been at home sleeping. Well, trying to sleep, anyway. Thoughts of Nate had haunted her all night. She smelled the faint aroma of chemicals on his skin when he walked up to her at the counter and closed her eyes to breathe it in. The euphoric high she experienced in the aftermath had nothing to do with the chemicals, though. It was all him. He breathed in the scent of her hair and exhaled slowly, like a predator savoring the anticipation of enjoying his prey. "I thought you might want to choose."

His lips skimmed her earlobe, and she swallowed. "Th-there are so many." How was she supposed to think straight when he was so close? And so naked, she thought as her eyes lowered and took in his smooth, sculpted chest. Other than a pair of low-slung, wash-worn denim cutoffs, he was sinfully bare from head to toe and beautiful everywhere her eyes landed. His nipples were as hard as hers were, but did they ache to be kissed and sucked the way hers did? "I . . . um . . . really like the black-and-white ones, but the c-color shots might look better in print. There won't be room f-for all of them, though."

"Four or five, at the most."

She went completely still as his tongue danced up one side of her neck and then dipped inside her ear. "Unless we expanded the article, m-maybe added another page or t-two."

He nipped at the skin on her neck, captured it between his teeth, and shook his head. "Too long," he said, his mouth on her ear. "Besides that, we've already sent Julia the text. It's too late to make changes to it before it hits the circuit. We have a week, at the most, before it goes viral."

She barely had time to enjoy the sensations shooting down her spine that his mouth on her ear caused before he dipped his head and went back to her neck, tongue dancing. "Oh." Her head lolled to one side to give him more access and her mouth fell open in delight. "W-well, we could do a piece on the d-dig."

"I'm going to let the university have the story. They'll use some of my shots and credit you with the find, though."

"That's good news." She was too disoriented with pleasure to be excited. Instead, she was on the verge of begging. Except for his busy mouth, he hadn't yet touched her and the waiting was driving her crazy. When he caged her in at the counter, she thought he was about to put her out of her misery, but he had other ideas.

"Very good news." His teeth sank into her earlobe and applied gentle, stinging pressure. "You smell almost as good as you taste."

The mention of his having tasted her activated the honey in her core, warming it to the boiling point. It coated her inner walls slowly, from the inside out, and tapped at the base of her hot button. A gasp shot out of her mouth. "You taste good, too."

"Taste me now."

She did. How could she resist? Her mouth

was open and on his nipple before she knew she wanted it to be. Her tongue flicked across the hard bud quickly, eliciting a strangled moan from him.

"Touch me, Tressie." She moved to the other nipple and slid the palms of her hands along his torso while she pleasured him and herself. He shuddered. "It isn't working, is it?" he whispered into her hair. "I thought after the first time that it would be enough, but it isn't, is it? Unfasten me, Tressie," he said without waiting for a response. "Take me out, take me in your hands and see how hard you make me."

She did. How could she not? Her hands were unzipping his shorts and pushing them down with a will of their own, trembling when they gripped him and squeezed. She pumped him slowly and experienced a moment's victory when his head fell back and he swore viciously. She took her mouth to the skin in the center of his chest and licked him there once and then twice. Then she reached up, sank her fingers into his hair and pulled his mouth down to hers.

Hell, no, it wasn't working. The more his tongue lapped against hers, the more she wanted of it and of him. And, still, nothing was touching between them, except their hungry mouths. Determined to remedy that, she turned the tables on him and issued a demand of her own. "Touch me, Nate."

It wouldn't last . . .

The fierce need to plunder and possess, the complete and utter surrender to sexual abandon, and the desire to exist for all time, buried in her tight, slick walls . . . it wouldn't last. It couldn't. Whatever this was that started happening to him when she was near, whatever this hold was that she seemed to have on him, it was temporary, an exquisite release from reality, meant only to be enjoyed in its season.

That's what Nate was telling himself when she peeled off her T-shirt and unhooked her bra. Those succulent breasts of hers swung free, and she slanted such an innocently knowing look up him that he couldn't resist cupping them, stroking the tips of her nipples until they sat up like juicy pieces of ripe fruit, beckoning his tongue. His mouth watered for them, and his penis expanded inside its velvety smooth sheath until his was an almost painful arousal.

No, this couldn't last. Their work here in Mercy was nearly finished. Their story had been submitted, and now there was nothing left to do but wait. They were almost out of moves to make on behalf of the town and, soon, they would go their separate ways. She would return to New York to try to revive her career, and he would accept one of the many assignment requests that Julia had been holding at bay in his absence. The likelihood that they would speak again, at least anytime soon, was slim to none. What would they have to discuss?

They hadn't talked about this at any length, what they were doing, and there would be no need to discuss it after it was over. He'd had his share of affairs over the years, some of them meaningful and more than a few of them meaningless, and this one would fall into one of those categories, just like all the rest. She would go back to gossiping for a living, and he would go back to despising what she did from afar. Perhaps every now and again he would slow down long enough to remember odd little details about her, like her infectious giggle and her thick, shiny hair, her slender hands and long fingers, and her nonstop chattering.

Maybe he would remember that he had invited her into his house, into his darkroom to see the pictures he had developed, and that he'd begun thinking about seducing her as soon as she'd walked through the door.

For once, she wasn't wearing stilettos and a flirty dress, just ordinary canvas sneakers and a T-shirt and shorts. Her face was bare of any makeup, and her skin glowed with health and a fine sheen of perspiration from her walk. He had taken one look at her, at the bright smile on her face, and completely forgotten that he was exhausted.

Maybe he would remember all that.

Maybe.

Reluctantly, Nate admitted to himself that there was so much more about Tressie Valentine that he would never forget.

The way she straddled him and rolled her hips around and around, just the way she was rolling them right now, was indelibly stamped on his brain. The way the muscles in her thighs flexed and bunched in unison with her inner muscles when she sat all the way down on his length was now a preference for him. The way her breasts swayed from side to side in front of his seeking mouth was positively hypnotizing. And the sounds she made while she was sinking down onto him and rising slowly to do it all over again was music to his ears.

His greedy hands gripped her ass, wanting to control her strokes and therefore control her influence over his own climax. But she pushed them away and planted her own hands in the center of his chest, rearing him back in the chair he was sitting in. Relinquishing control, he took his hands to her breasts and left them there as she rode him into blissful oblivion.

A long time later, he carried her over to the futon that he had set up against the far wall in his darkroom for the times that he was too exhausted to find his bed, and he laid her down. Half-asleep already, she curled up in a fetal position on the thick cushion and watched him from under heavy eyelids. A shy smile curved her lips and stole his breath. Wanting to capture and immortalize it, he moved away slowly and dimmed the lights.

Then he picked up his camera.

CHAPTER 7

After two days of looking from afar for fear of getting in the way, Tressie said to hell with it and ventured onto Moira's property to take a closer look at what the archaeological students were doing. From what Nate had already told her, she knew that the site had been authenticated not long after the team had arrived a week ago, but other than looking from a distance and speculating on what was happening, she had no clue about how the work was progressing.

He had agreed to allow the university complete control over the project and was giving them a wide berth, but Tressie didn't share his nonchalant attitude. No doubt he had seen and done all kinds of things during his career, so this was probably just another important event to add to his list of been there–done thats. She, on the other hand, had never experienced anything like it.

The ground over the hidden room near the creek had been excavated, baring the space to the world and allowing Tressie to see as she got closer to the roped-off area that it was larger than she and Nate had originally thought. In the light of day, she could make out the frame of the opening to the underground tunnel that had once led to the main house, and she could see where water had leaked into the room in some places. The artifacts that she and Nate had discovered had been removed and were now lying on a plastic tarp on the ground a few feet away. A student was working with them, and she stopped to watch him.

That's where she was when Moira found her. She appeared at Tressie's shoulder suddenly, without warning, leaning heavily on an intricately carved wooden cane and sporting one of the wide-brimmed hats that she was legendary for. Dark sunglasses hid her eyes, but there was no mistaking the warm smile on her face when she turned to Tressie and laid a soft hand on her arm.

"I was wondering when you would come and see for yourself what you started," Moira said. "It's a little overwhelming, isn't it? All these people, all this activity. It's been years since I've had this many people at my house at one time, if ever."

By Tressie's count, there had to be at least fifty people milling around the grounds. Factoring in the equipment that they'd brought with them, she had to admit that it did look like a small-scale takeover was in progress. At the other end of the grounds, past the house and the flower gardens, a row of trailers were parked on the grass, and on the end where the digging was going on, a row of portable lavatories had been set up. She couldn't even begin to imagine what the project was costing the university. "I bet you can't wait for all this to be over with."

"Oh, no, on the contrary — it's just the opposite. I'm having fun." A soft giggle bubbled out of Moira's mouth. "At night, some of the students come out of the trailers, pitch huge tents around the creek and sit out here under the moon, singing and playing the guitar. They sound like they're having so much fun and, I'll tell you what, if I were a few years younger, I'd be right out there with them. I'll be sad to see them go, to tell you the truth."

"Are they almost done?" Tressie would be sad to see them go, too. Their presence in town had done a lot for morale. Not many residents had actually come in person to see what was happening, but word had quickly spread. The excitement in the air was tangible and, for the first time in a long time, people had something positive to talk about. For the time being, the eminent domain crisis had taken a backseat to the possibility that, as Jasper Holmes had put to Tressie just this morning, Harriet Tubman might have once traveled through Mercy, Georgia. The very idea had put a sparkle in the old man's eye that Tressie had never seen there or anywhere else before. Sadly, when the students left, the crisis would once again overshadow everything and everyone.

"They have at least another couple of weeks' worth of work to do here," Moira guessed. "But everything is happening so fast — time is passing so quickly. It'll all be over with before we know it." She fell silent, her attention momentarily caught by a tattered leather-bound book that the student on the ground in front of them was gently dusting off. The bowl that Tressie had almost touched that first night was there, too, as was a bundle of what looked like handkerchiefs or rags. After the bowl had been dusted off, he turned his attention to the bundle and began gently untangling it. Moira leaned closer to Tressie and stage-whispered, "I assume Nathaniel told you that he's giving the university all rights to the findings from the dig?"

"Yes, he mentioned it." Still unsure of how she felt about Nate's decision, Tressie decided not to elaborate any further. If Moira was in favor of the decision, the last thing she wanted to do was put her foot in her mouth.

"You have to respect his generosity," Moira said, nodding sagely. "But I think, if there was ever a time to be selfish, this is it." Surprised, Tressie stared at Moira. "What? You think I don't realize the impact that this could have on Gwinnet County's final decision? We won't have another useless town hall meeting for weeks and by then we could really give them something to think about." She took a deep breath and released it slowly, scanning the view spread out in front of her. "I'm afraid the story the two of you wrote won't be enough."

"But this might be," Tressie put in quietly. "If this and the room in your cellar are true stops along the Underground Railroad, that means that your house and your land are historical landmarks." Tressie searched Moira's eyes for confirmation. Finding none, she literally wilted. "Doesn't it?"

"That awful company — Consolidated Investments, isn't it? — is already aware of that. They've graciously offered to build

141

around my property and allow me to stay. As if I should be grateful to have a home while the rest of town is plowed down and people are scattered to the winds like ashes."

Tressie thought about the purchase-offer documents that she had been carrying around in her purse for the past two days. Aside from accessing her email, printing them out and tucking them inside her purse, she hadn't done anything with them. The longer she remained in Mercy, the guiltier she felt about even wanting to accept the offer, let alone actually going through with it.

She hadn't come back to Mercy to get all tangled up in humanitarian efforts, and now that she was, she desperately wanted to see the town prevail. After everything it had been through, it deserved to win. The thought of selling her land to the opposition made her feel like a traitor and, much like what Nate had said about his late mother, her own grandmother wouldn't be at all pleased to know what she'd done. Ma'Dear wouldn't have dreamed of selling out, no matter how much money was on the table for the taking.

But Ma'Dear hadn't had the responsibilities that Tressie had. Nor had she ever dreamed of a life beyond teaching children the difference between verbs and adverbs. Tressie wanted so much more than the quiet, simple life Ma'Dear had lived. In fact, she didn't want a quiet, simple life at all. She wanted the freedom to allow Vanessa Valentino to write what she wanted, when she wanted, where she wanted, all while enjoying the stability that a financial nest egg would provide. After everything Vanessa Valentino had been through recently, she deserved to win, too.

Mercy was a nice place to visit, but she never planned to call the place home again. If she didn't sell to Norman Harper, then she would just sell to someone else. So why shouldn't she get the highest return on her property? If the town was bulldozed to the ground and wiped off the map, which was exactly what she feared was going to happen anyway, then what difference would it make in the long run?

"At least that's something," Tressie told Moira. "You get to keep your house and your land. That's good news."

"It's not about me or even you, Tressie. It's about right and wrong." One of the rags that the student unraveled had spots of what Tressie could only assume was dried blood on it. He held it up to the sun, studied it for a long moment and then set it aside to

143

write something in the notebook that was lying open at his side. Moira watched him thoughtfully for several seconds before she spoke again. "Did you know that this town was named Mercy because the freed slaves who first settled here believed that God had finally shown them mercy?"

"No, I didn't know that."

"It stands to reason, though, doesn't it? And now the state is showing the town no mercy.

"It makes me so angry." She lifted her hand from Tressie's arm long enough to slip her sunglasses off. Staring into Tressie's eyes, she asked, "Have they made you an offer to sell your grandmother's house and land, Tressie?"

Under the steady glare of Moira's probing green eyes, Tressie didn't even consider lying. "Yes, but I . . . uh . . . haven't quite decided yet. I came here planning to, but now . . ." She shrugged helplessly and looked away. "Now I don't know."

Nodding slowly, Moira seemed to accept her answer for what it was. "It would certainly be the easiest way, I guess," she eventually replied, and suddenly Tressie felt two inches tall and transparent.

Done with the rags for the time being, the student began handling the leather-bound book. When he carefully cracked it open with gloved hands, Tressie saw that it was some sort of children's storybook, and her heart melted. "Some poor child probably accidentally left that behind," she speculated.

"More likely, someone was using it to teach others how to read and write," Moira corrected. "At some stops, runaways were hidden for days, sometimes weeks before moving on to the next stop."

"Do you think there are more stops here in town?"

"I doubt it. I imagine that this area was mostly foliage back then. There may have been one or two other plantations nearby, but not much else." She smiled at the student, slipped her sunglasses back over her eyes and took Tressie's elbow with her free hand. "I think I'd better get out of the sun for a while. Come, join me for lunch."

It wasn't a request, and Tressie didn't dare refuse. She helped Moira cross the lawn to the main house and, at Moira's direction, followed her through the French doors into a large, sunny kitchen. A maid was chopping vegetables at a center island and glancing at a television that was set up on a nearby counter. She looked up when they entered, smiled and went back to her task.

"Lunch is coming right up, Miss Moira," she sang cheerfully, still chopping. At a commercial break, she tore her eyes away from the television set and focused on Tressie. "Hello, there. I'm Janice."

"Hi, I'm Tressie," Tressie said as she pulled a chair away from the kitchen table for Moira. After Moira was seated and Tressie was certain that she wasn't in danger of slipping and fracturing anything, she returned Janice's smile. "Whatever that is you're cooking smells delicious."

Janice glowed at the compliment. "Oh, it's just a little pasta salad recipe that I made up.

"The secret," she declared with a flourish of the knife in her hand, "is in the sauce. It's a little spicy, a little sweet." She transferred the celery and carrots that she'd been chopping to a metal strainer, then turned toward the sink behind her. Over the running water, she added, "Have a seat and make yourself comfortable. I'll get you two something cool to drink in just a second. It must be ninety degrees outside."

"Closer to a hundred," Moira said, pulling a neatly folded handkerchief from her bosom and dabbing at her face and neck. Sighing, she looked up at Tressie and waved her into a chair. "Sit down, dear. She says lunch will be ready shortly, but it'll be at least until *Another World* goes off before we even see so much as a buttered roll. You might as well relax in the meantime."

Tressie smothered a giggle when Janice shot Moira a sidelong glance and rolled her eyes to the ceiling. "I don't think I've ever been inside of your house before, Miss Moira. It's beautiful," she said, looking around the spotless state-of-the-art kitchen admiringly. She seated herself in the chair across the table from Moira and folded her hands in her lap.

"Thank you. Once, I thought I would fill it with lots and lots of children, but it never happened. I had to settle for filling it with my husbands' children, instead. I had three husbands and three stepchildren, so that worked for a time, but after they were all grown, it was just me again. Do you have children, Tressie?"

"Ah . . . no," Tressie said and laughed. "I don't think I'm ready for them just yet. There's still so much that I want to do before I take on that challenge."

"Time waits for no one, dear. I'm living proof of that." She reached for the tall glass that Janice set in front of her as soon as it hit the table, and took a sip of iced tea. "You live in New York, right? I think I remember

Juanita mentioning something about you working for a newspaper there."

Tressie sipped her own iced tea while she formulated a response. "I did work for a newspaper there, but I don't anymore. We . . . uh . . . decided to part ways. But I do still live in New York."

"So you're unemployed right now?"

"I'm on hiatus."

"Same thing," Moira pronounced with a flippant wave of her hand. "Ah, here's lunch, thank God." They sat back as Janice set out linen-wrapped silverware, a basket of steaming rolls and a butter dish, and then slid heaping plates of cold pasta salad tossed with grilled tenderloin strips in front of them. When she had moved away again, Moira unwrapped her silverware and shook out her napkin, settling it on her lap. "My stepson is in newspapers, too. You two should meet. You've heard of Miles Dixon?"

Tressie nearly dropped her fork. Had she heard of Miles Dixon? The question should've been, who *hadn't* heard of Miles Dixon? The fact that he had been the one to write the first and, as far as she knew, only authorized biography of Pamela Mayes was well-known, but it was also pretty much irrelevant in light of the fact that he was even more well-known as a media-industry powerhouse. Tressie had long since lost count of the number of newspapers and magazine publishing houses that Miles Dixon either owned outright or owned shares in around the world. Unfortunately, the *Inquisitor* wasn't one of them, so the man probably had no idea that she existed. With Moira's help, though, maybe one day soon he would.

She hoped she wasn't gushing when she said, "Yes, I've heard of him and I'd love to meet him."

"Good, then we'll have to arrange it. I've been meaning to call him, anyway. It occurs to me that he's due for a visit and the timing of things here couldn't be more perfect. Putting him and Nathaniel together right now and seeing what they can come up with between them ought to be interesting, don't you think?"

"It certainly can't hurt," Tressie agreed as she buttered a roll. "To tell you the truth, Moira, I've been thinking about the piece that Nate and I have been working on and —"

"It won't be enough, as I said earlier," Moira cut in, and Tressie sighed with relief at having been rescued from saying it herself. "We need to do more and quickly."

"I think you might be right. Even if the

story goes viral, which I'm sure it will with Nate's name and his contacts backing it, there's still no guarantee that it will sway the state one way or the other. I think we need to do something that's really going to make an impression on them, something that celebrates the town's heritage and makes them understand how important this place is to the people who live here at the same time. Our story is meant to do that, but if we can do more, it would help a lot."

Moira bit into a roll and chewed thoughtfully. "Then we'll have to make sure that whatever we do will complement the article, and ensure further success."

So this was what it was like, Nate thought as he paced the floor in front of the picture window in his living room. This was what it was like to watch and wait for a woman. In all his damn near forty years, he'd never been reduced to this kind of nonsense. And now that he had, he couldn't say that he cared for it even a little bit.

He stopped in front of the window and peeked out the blinds for the hundredth time, grunting impatiently when he didn't see anything or anyone on the street. Where the hell was she? Almost twelve hours had passed since they'd parted ways after breakfast at Hayden's Diner early this morning, and she'd been missing in action ever since. She wasn't answering her cell phone, she hadn't called him and she hadn't responded to any of the fifteen text messages that he'd sent her. In a few hours it would be dark out and, among other things, he was starving.

Eyeing the rolled-up blanket, candles and crystal candleholders sitting in the middle of the floor — the last of the items to be added to the picnic basket that he'd packed earlier — he went back to the window and peeked again. Still no sign of her.

He was debating whether or not to go looking for her when his cell phone rang. Thinking that it was her, hoping that it was her, he went to his bedroom and snatched it up from the nightstand without bothering to check the caller ID. "Where the hell are you?"

"Um . . . I'm sorry, maybe I've dialed the wrong number."

Recognizing Julia's voice immediately, Nate sat on the side of the bed and threaded his fingers through his hair. He took a breath for patience while he searched for a reasonably friendly tone. "Sorry, Julia. I thought you were someone else."

"Clearly," Julia drawled, a hint of laughter

in her voice. "Is this a bad time?"

Hell, yes, it's a bad time. I'm in the middle of driving myself insane, wondering when and if a woman that I shouldn't even be involved with in the first place is coming to meet me tonight. I don't much care about anything else right now.

Aloud, he said, "It's never a bad time for you, sugar. What's on your mind?"

"Your itinerary, for starters. Beasley over at CNN was able to move some things around and get you in for a twenty-minute interview this Friday."

As preoccupied as he was, it took a few seconds for Julia's words to sink in. "Friday, as in tomorrow?"

"I know it's last-minute, but he wanted you on the Friday-night around-the-nation segment with one or the other of those Gumbel brothers, and since they're also doing a segment on New Orleans almost a decade after Katrina, the timing is right. And . . ."

She was silent for an excruciatingly long time while she shuffled through papers and typed on her keyboard. All Nate could think about was lemon-pepper fried chicken and potato salad — which he had won the right to browbeat Jasper Holmes into making for him after a particularly nerve-racking chess game today — and the fruit bowls that he planned to hand-feed Tressie from, and the slightly tart, slightly sweet white wine that he hoped Tressie would drink enough of to let him lick every ounce of the fruit dip off her gorgeous breasts.

And speaking of her gorgeous breasts, where the hell was she?

"And . . ." he prompted Julia when the silence stretched on.

"Oh, sorry," she said, laughing. "I was just double-checking your itinerary. What was I saying? Oh, now I remember. I was saying that the Friday-night segment actually works out great for you, because I've also scheduled you for prerecorded interviews with Barbara Walters — that's Friday afternoon — and Diane Sawyer — that's Saturday morning. I'm still waiting to hear back from Anderson Cooper's camp, but these engagements should keep you busy in the meantime and get the ball rolling."

He opened his mouth to speak just as the sound of the front door opening and closing reached his ears.

"I've booked you a seat in first class on a flight out of Atlanta first thing in the morning, and I managed to get you your usual suite at the Plaza," Julia went on. "You should land in New York by ten and have a few hours to relax before they send a driver to fetch you. Is your fax machine on?"

Every atom in his body was poised to hear the sound of footsteps. Hearing none, he stood and took the phone with him to the living room. "I'm sorry, what?" he said when he realized that Julia had just asked him a question.

"I asked you if your fax machine was turned on."

He turned the corner into the living room and stopped short. "Uh . . . yeah, it's . . ." There she was. He forgot all about being hungry for food and wondered if she would let him suck on her lips instead.

"All right, I'll fax your itinerary over to you now."

"Fine, just . . . fine." He hung up in the middle of whatever Julia was saying and dropped his phone somewhere in the vicinity of the blanket on the floor. "I've been calling you all day," he said as he advanced on Tressie. "Where the hell have you been?" Wherever she'd been, she looked great. Her skin was still glowing from the sun, as if it had been kissed all over by light, and her hair was slightly windblown. Instead of one of her signature sundresses, she wore a colorful sarong-style miniskirt, a sleeveless denim shirt that she had knotted above her belly button, and matching espadrilles on her feet. As usual, she managed to look effortlessly put together.

"With Moira. I went to see how the dig was going and —"

He tried not to snatch at her, but she still landed against his chest breathlessly, staring up at him as if he'd lost his mind. And maybe he had, he thought as he licked his way inside her mouth quickly and possessively. The instant her lips parted, he sank his tongue in her mouth as far as possible and instantly took the kiss into deep and wet territory. His hands went to the bare skin around her waist and squeezed, while his mouth devoured hers greedily.

Check yourself, Nate, he told himself. *Keep this up and you'll swallow her whole.* Still, he kept kissing her until he'd had his fill. Breaking the kiss slowly, he stared down into her wide eyes and saw his own wide-eyed, stunned gaze mirrored there.

So, okay, maybe he was a little insane.

Clearly taken by surprise, Tressie took a step back from him, steadied herself and ran her fingers through her hair. "I ended up staying for lunch with Moira, and after that we sat on the back veranda and talked. My phone was off," she said by way of explanation. "I didn't turn it back on until after I'd left Moira. I came right over when I saw that you'd called —"

"About a hundred times," Nate supplied, suddenly feeling more than a little ridiculous.

"Something like that." Her smile was slightly coy as she tried to scoot around him. "I thought there might've been a fire here or some other life-or-death emergency."

"Very funny." She stepped around him only to look up and find him right there, in her face and ready to grab her up and kiss her senseless again, a quiet admission on the tip of his tongue. "I missed you."

Apparently, it was exactly the right thing to say. The teasing glint in her eyes disappeared and Tressie softened visibly all over. "Oh," she breathed, running her palms up and down his chest slowly and looking everywhere but at him. He'd never seen a woman look so beautiful when she blushed. "I missed you a little, too."

Her eyes flickered up to his long enough for him to see what was on her mind — lovemaking, deep and wet kisses, skin on skin, friction and heat — before she looked away again. He sucked in a sharp breath, felt his penis stir in his pants and dipped his head in search of her mouth again. "Just a little?"

"Well, maybe a little more than just a little bit." He was less than an inch away from laying another kiss on her when she suddenly noticed the items stacked on the floor. She reared back and leaned sideways to get a better look. "What's all this?"

"The makings of a picnic," he said, sniffing at the lavender-scented skin of her neck.

"Oooh," she cooed, "I love picnics."

He bit into her earlobe lightly, right next to the diamond stud there. "I thought you might, which is why I planned one for today."

"So what are we waiting on? Where's the food?"

Now it was his turn to step back and stare at her. "Don't you think it's a little dark out in Truman's Field for a picnic, sugar?"

"So? We'll have a picnic right here." Suddenly excited, Tressie kicked off her shoes and hopped around the room like a child. "You go get the food. Wait, you do have food, don't you?"

"Of course, but —"

"Good. You go get it and I'll set up everything in here. This is one time when the absence of furniture is a plus." She looked up from shaking out the blanket and saw that he was still standing there, watching her. "What are you waiting for, Nate? Go on." She went back to hopping around excitedly. "I love picnics."

In the few minutes that it took him to rescue the picnic basket from the refrigerator and bring it into the living room, she had spread out the blanket, set up the candles in the candleholders and lit them. All that was left to do was dim the lights, which he took care of before he kicked off his leather sandals and joined her on the blanket.

"All we're missing now is some music to set the mood," Tressie said, watching Nate unpack the wine and begin unscrewing the cork.

"I was hoping," he said as he filled a wineglass and handed it to her, "that we could make some music of our own." His eyes flickered up to hers and held. "After I feed you, of course, because you will definitely need your strength to hit the high notes that I have planned for you, sugar."

Her skin warmed even more in the candlelight, and an angelic smile curved her lips. "Well, then, you'd better make me a plate."

Later, after the picnic had moved from the living room to the bedroom and Nate had feasted on Tressie until they were both damp with perspiration and struggling to catch their breath, he collapsed on the bed beside her and flirted with the idea of drifting off to sleep. He'd lost count of the number of times that his eyes had rolled to the back of his head or his toes had curled so hard that he'd heard bones popping, and now his entire body was in a state of orgasmic shock.

Could a grown man die from experiencing so many intense, mind-numbing, euphoria-inducing orgasms that it almost hurt to feel so good? He hadn't had time to consider the question at any length before, but now he was seriously wondering if it was a real possibility.

One thing was for damn sure, he thought as he summoned the strength to reach for the covers and pull them up over the both of them. She had pulled the old switcheroo on him, and he hadn't seen it coming until it was too late to turn the tables back around on her. By then she was already riding him, fast and hard, and he couldn't have denied himself the pleasure of feeling her hot, tight, spasming body bouncing up and down on his length, wrapped around him like a slick fist, if it had meant the difference between going to heaven or hell.

At some point he had gotten his wish, and

now he knew that sweet, creamy fruit dip was completely wasted on fruit. Not only had the stuff tasted incredible as a topping on Tressie's tight nipples, but it had tasted even better as he was licking and sucking the last of it from her swollen, pulsing button. For his efforts, she had come long and hard, vibrating like a live wire and calling out his name, and then she'd fallen completely silent and gone completely still when he'd braced himself over her and driven every inch of his throbbing shaft into her over and over again.

He hadn't been expecting her to want more, to need more, but she had, and he'd had to dig deep to give it to her. He was searching for his breath and having trouble finding it, still inexplicably hard as steel when she climbed on top of him and took him in again. Her slippery walls milked him dry, until he had uttered a sound that was equivalent to waving a white flag, rolled her over to the mattress and emptied himself into her for the third and final time.

Any more and she would've killed him.

And he would've gladly let her.

"Oh, my God," Tressie panted for what must have been the thousandth time since they had landed in bed. "I mean . . . wow." She giggled throatily and reached out to run a hand down Nate's back. "I can't feel my legs," she said, full-out laughing now, "and I need them to carry me to the shower. Unless you want to carry me . . ."

"Not a chance," Nate drawled, serious as a heart attack. He was having problems connecting with the nerves in his own legs at the moment. If he tried to carry her, they would both probably end up in traction, if, that is, one of them was able to crawl to a phone and call for help. "I need every ounce of my remaining strength to get to the shower myself, and then after that I need to pack. I won't have time to do it in the morning."

Tressie's head popped up off the pillow. "Pack? Where are you going?"

"I thought I mentioned it to you." Hadn't he? "I'm leaving in the morning."

CHAPTER 8

Was that her heart dropping to her stomach? No, no, it wasn't. That was her heart jumping up into her throat.

"No, you didn't mention it."

"Oh." He had the nerve to look genuinely puzzled. "I thought I did."

She watched him peel himself away from the bed and stroll into the bathroom as if what he had just said to her was no big deal. Which, she supposed, it really wasn't. Unless you counted the fact that they had been seeing each other steadily for the past month or so and had been lovers for nearly as long. Was it unreasonable to expect him to share things with her every once in a while? Apparently so, if his nonchalant attitude was any indication. But what about the attitude that she suddenly had? Didn't it count for something?

Wait a minute. Maybe some objectivity was called for here. Yes, they were lovers, but neither of them had gone into the situation with any expectations. So why did she expect anything from him now? As far as summertime flings went, she had to admit that this one had been a scorcher, but that's exactly what it was — a summertime fling. When it was over, he would go his way and she hers. She'd always understood that. But still, if this was his way of telling her that the affair had run its course, it left a hell of a lot to be desired.

She wasn't quite sure how she felt. Was she angry? Hurt? Disappointed? What? With so many emotions churning around inside her, it was hard to pinpoint exactly which one took precedence. Foolishly, she'd thought that, when the time came for them to part ways, it would happen differently, more meaningfully, as if they had actually come to mean something to one another. Not like this — not with a casual "I'm leaving" and nothing more.

God, how stupid was she? Had she really thought that something more than a good time would come out of this? I mean, she was dealing with the infamous Nathaniel Woodberry, wasn't she? Tressie could no more see him settling down with one woman than she could see herself venturing into the jungles of Cuba to hunt down a story.

The images just didn't jell — neither of them — and they never would.

Play it cool, Tressie. No need to let him see how discombobulated you are right now.

None of the sophisticated women in movies lose their cool when an affair goes south, so you shouldn't, either. Shake it off and get your head back in the game, would you?

She cleared her throat and swallowed the lump.

"How long will you be gone?"

He hadn't volunteered that information and he should have. At least, she thought he should've. It had been quite some time since she'd been in an intimate relationship with a man, but some things were a given. Was he leaving Mercy for good or . . . ? Feeling exposed for reasons that she couldn't quite name, she sat up in bed and wrapped the sheet around her to wait for his answer.

"No more than a couple of days," Nate said from the depths of the bathroom. The shower switched on full blast, and his voice rose to be heard over it. "I have a couple of interviews scheduled in New York. After that, I'll be back. I told you about the interviews, didn't I?"

Yes, the interviews. He had mentioned those, she remembered, and released the breath she didn't know she'd been holding

164

until just then. Television news interviews about Mercy, Georgia, and what was going on here. Right. A few days. Okay.

"Are you coming in with me or should I save you some hot water?"

She looked up and saw him leaning in the bathroom doorway, gloriously naked and peering into the semidarkness of the bedroom at her, and thought, *Uh-oh.* Just the sight of him caused her heart rate to pick up and goose bumps to pop up all over her skin. A telltale surge snaked through her belly and made a beeline for that sensitive little bud between her thighs. Her reaction to him was instinctive, like a reflex that she couldn't control, and it wasn't showing any signs of weakening as time went on. If anything, it had only gotten stronger.

As if a lightbulb had suddenly come on in her head, she saw herself clearly just then and didn't like the image staring back at her at all. How in the world, she wondered with something like an awestruck expression on her face, had she managed to fall half in love with the world's most confirmed bachelor? Then again, how could she not have? Here they were, in this godforsaken little town together, with nothing to do but be with each other day in and day out. What else was she supposed to do but lose her heart and, apparently, her common sense in the process?

This was bad. This was really, *really* bad.

Maybe his leaving for a couple of days was a good thing. The time apart would give her the space to clear her head and decide what her next move would be. She'd always known that she wouldn't stay in Mercy forever and, really, she was starting to feel that she'd been here too long already. Maybe it was time to think about returning to New York and putting all her energy into rebuilding some sort of career for herself.

Maybe . . .

"Tressie?"

Since she'd been in Mercy, she had let it all fall by the wayside — her career aspirations, her obligations and responsibilities back in New York, the sale of Ma'Dear's house and land, everything. Now, with his announcement that he was carrying on with the details of his life, came a reminder that she needed to get back to carrying on with the details of her own life. This was an affair, plain and simple, and if there were any feelings involved, she was sure they were purely one-sided. The mistake in getting too attached, too dependent on the here and now, was all hers, and now she needed to get started on rectifying it.

First thing tomorrow, she promised herself as she unwrapped herself from the sheet and got to her feet. First thing tomorrow she would get started . . . after he was gone and she didn't have to look at him, hear him, feel him and want, want, want.

He wasn't gone for a few days, he was gone for a week.

Tressie caught herself hovering around her cell phone, waiting for it to ring, the first night he was gone.

She caught herself doing the same thing, only this time *willing* the thing to ring, the second night he was gone.

Then on the third day that he was away, she reminded herself that she and Nate weren't committed to each other and that he wasn't obligated to call her. There was no reason for her to feel a little hurt because her cell phone was stubbornly silent, and there was no reason to sit around moping about it.

But she did.

His interviews had gone exceptionally well. She knew because she'd been watching on her laptop and marveling at his seemingly effortless camera presence. She'd seen him on television before, but this time was somehow different. More than ever before, she noticed the way his sleepy eyes sparkled and seduced the camera. The way his smile was all sex, liquid and knowing in a way that caused her to shift in her seat more than once. He was a magnificent-looking man in the broken-in jeans, T-shirts and Italian leather sandals that he practically lived in here in Mercy. But in the tailored blazers, collarless shirts and wire-rimmed glasses that he'd worn during his interviews, he was drop-dead gorgeous.

It was easy to be distracted by his good looks, but even those couldn't overshadow his obvious intelligence. He had spoken about the situation in Mercy eloquently and succinctly, providing both facts and folklore, and discussing at length the piece that they had put together. When the discovery of the Underground Railroad stop came up, he provided voice-over for a brief video that had been provided by the university and, again, stressed the significance of the town's history. In the wake of the interviews, Tressie was impressed with him all over again and, once again, reminded that her time in Mercy and her time with Nate was winding up.

And, still, he didn't call.

It wasn't as if she didn't have things to do to keep her busy, she told herself, because she did. Determined to take her mind off him and the void that his absence had suddenly created, she occupied herself by setting up her workshop out on the sunporch and spending time online, creating a new and improved weblog for the relaunch of the Vanessa Valentino name and brand. She even brainstormed a list of ideas for possible story leads, did some preliminary research that seemed promising and sketched out a few possible logo design ideas.

After that, she made some calls and arranged for the items that she had packed and moved from Ma'Dear's house to go to a local storage facility and be donated to charity. The only items left in the house were a few essential kitchen tools, the kitchen table and her old bedroom furniture, and she arranged to have those things picked up for donation, too. With the house finally and completely empty, she scratched one more thing off her to-do list. By day four of no-word-from-Nate, she was settled in a room at the Mercy Hotel and back to eating takeout from Hayden's Diner for breakfast, lunch and dinner.

On Thursday she had lunch again with Moira, but this time they did more than just talk about putting their heads together for change. They had spent most of their time together discussing the town fair that took place in Truman's Field every summer. This summer, with everything else going on, plans for the annual fair had fallen by the wayside, but Moira had taken it upon herself to get the ball rolling again, thinking that it would be just what the town needed to boost morale. With Tressie's help, they had come up with a step-by-step plan for taking care of the million-and-one details that went into planning such an event. Around midnight, when Tressie had finally said her goodbyes and left, Moira was ready to begin making the necessary arrangements. Tressie had purposely held back from getting too deeply involved in carrying out the event, because she wasn't quite sure if she would still be in town then. As she'd told Moira, her reasons for hanging around were becoming fewer and fewer, especially since she had finally decided to decline Norman Harper's offer.

It took her a while to realize that she'd been carrying around the offer documents in her purse like a security blanket, but when she finally did, guilt swamped her all over again. As much as she wanted to feel disconnected from the town and its people, after spending so much time here, it just wasn't possible. Selling her property and land to Consolidated Investments felt too much like selling out, even if she did desperately need the money. The house held a lot of good memories for her and she thought that maybe, after the town had survived its current crisis and moved on, another family could move into it and create more good memories. Ma'Dear would've wanted that.

So, for the time being, she would keep the house and she would just have to come up with some other way to pull herself up by the bootstraps and carry on. If the people of Mercy could do it, then so could she.

It hadn't been an easy decision, but if she was wondering if it was the right one, she got her answer Friday morning when she wandered onto Moira's property again to see how the dig was going.

At this point, the student archaeologists were busy sifting through the newly turned earth surrounding the original outdoor dig site. Under the watchful eyes of supervising professors, they were making sure that they weren't overlooking any important details in what had turned out to be an exhaustive analysis of the grounds behind Moira's house. Walking slowly and carefully, Tressie surveyed the damage and wondered how long it would take for the grass to grow back and Moira's meticulously tended flower beds to recuperate from the abuse. Moira must've been wondering the same thing, Tressie thought as she spotted the woman in the distance. She was leaning on a man's arm and pointing the tip of her cane at a recently turned section of dirt. From the way the man's head was bobbing in agreement, it was obvious that she wasn't pleased with what she was looking at. Tressie walked up behind them just as Moira was pushing the tip of the cane back into the ground.

"Well, I guess there's nothing that can be done about it now, but, still . . ." Moira was saying. She reached up and pushed her straw hat down more securely on her head and caught sight of Tressie in her peripheral vision. She spun around as quickly as the cane would allow, a wide smile on her face. "Oh, Tressie! I'm so glad you're here! I was going to call you this evening, but this is even better."

"I'm sorry to just show up like this," Tressie said, moving closer and grasping the hand that Moira extended to her. "I guess I just can't stay away from the dig site. I'm so fascinated by it."

"Who said you should stay away?" Moira wanted to know. "You know you're welcome to visit anytime." She looked up at the man at her side. "Dear, this is Tressie Valentine, the woman who discovered the underground room and set all this in motion. You remember me telling you about her."

Tressie didn't recognize the tall, thin man standing next to Moira, though there was something vaguely familiar about him, but she smiled warmly at him anyway. He had short, curly brown hair, curious brown eyes and an easygoing smile that she liked immediately. "It's a pleasure to meet you," she said, releasing Moira's hand to take the one he offered.

"I believe the pleasure's all mine," he said, looking slightly amused. "It's not every day that one gets to meet the notoriously nosy Vanessa Valentino in person. Until just recently, I'd pictured you as a wrinkled little gray-haired lady with balls of steel." He noticed the expression on Moira's face and the narrowed gaze that she aimed at him and did a double take. "What?"

Moira shook her head slowly, her eyes speaking volumes. "You know I don't like talk like that. The last time I checked, there was nothing wrong with wrinkled little gray-haired ladies."

"Nothing at all, sweetheart. Nothing at all." Still looking amused, he released Tressie's hand, then leaned down and pressed an indulgent kiss to Moira's cheek, making her brighten instantly. Then he straightened and pinned Tressie with a knowing gaze. "Word on the street is that the good folks over at the *Inquisitor* cut you loose after the story you did on Gary Price blew up in their faces."

Speechless, Tressie felt her mouth working, but couldn't seem to make it produce sound. Had he just called her out publicly as Vanessa Valentino? How in the world did he know who she was? And how had he heard about her being suspended from the *Inquisitor*? Did everyone know? Suddenly, she was rethinking her decision not to sell to Consolidated Investments. If word truly was on the street, as he said, and everyone who was anyone now knew that she was Vanessa Valentino, her career was over and done with regardless what she did to try and revive it. She'd need all the money she could get her hands on just to survive at least until she found another career path and, with her professional reputation preceding her, who knew how long that would be.

"You're wondering how I know who you are," he said, reading the look on her face like a book.

"Um, yes," Tressie managed to get out.

"Yes, as a matter of fact, I am." She'd never even told Moira. Had Nate?

"Oh, goodness!" Moira piped up, flushing visibly. "Where are my manners? Tressie, dear, this is my stepson, Miles Dixon. You remember me telling you about him."

Tressie released a long breath that she would've been embarrassed about if she hadn't been so busy feeling a rush of relief instead. Now she knew why he looked so familiar to her and how he knew who she was. Or who she used to be, as the case was. Where the media was concerned, there was probably very little that he didn't know or couldn't find out. If Donald Trump was the man in the business world, then Miles Dixon was *that guy* in the news arena.

Remembering Moira's mention of arranging a meeting between her and Miles, Tressie sent the woman a grateful smile, thinking that her timing couldn't have been better. A new job would give her even more to look forward to after she left Mercy.

"Well, then, I guess I should just go ahead and confirm the rumors," Tressie said, wondering how bad she'd look if she simply threw herself at Miles's feet and begged for a job. "I was —"

"No need," he interrupted, still smiling. "I've followed your columns for a while now and, to tell you the truth, I was wondering why you were wasting your talent with them anyway. A gossip column is okay for a time, and there is an audience for something like that, but you'd be doing yourself a disservice by limiting yourself to sticking your nose in other people's business exclusively."

Tressie didn't know whether to feel insulted or complimented. "Actually, I was planning to continue the Vanessa Valentino column on my own."

"And then what?" he asked pointedly. "Give it a few more years and someone might step up with even more connections than you, and be willing to jump into the spotlight instead of hiding behind fake names, and you'll be a has-been. What will you do then?"

"Vanessa Valentino is more than just a gossip columnist," Tressie sputtered indignantly. She was beginning to see why Miles was so successful in the industry. He was borderline insensitive. "She's a franchise. Or she will be by the time I'm done with her."

"Not if you have any hope of working for me."

"But I have a following and I've already begun setting the stage for a comeback."

"Well, then, good luck with that. Let me

know how it turns out."

Not only was he insensitive, but he was an ass, too. "Thank you. I will."

Moira's flowery laugh eased into the middle of the tension that had suddenly sprung up between them. "Isn't this working out well?" she asked, looking as though she knew good and well that it wasn't. Her eyes darted across Tressie's tight expression and then jumped over to Miles's placid one. "I had a feeling that you two would work well together."

"Let's not get ahead of ourselves," Tressie couldn't help saying. "Mr. Dixon and I don't exactly seem to be making a love connection, Moira."

"Sure we are," he said, positioning himself between Tressie and Moira and turning the three of them toward the main house. "As a matter of fact, I think I have a position in one of my New York offices that would fit you perfectly, Tressie. It's a relatively small paper and I just recently acquired it, but I have big plans for it."

Tressie slanted a wary look up at him. Should she or shouldn't she? In the end, her curiosity won out and she heard herself asking, "Which paper is it?" before she could stop herself.

"The *Manhattan Style Report.*"

As if he hadn't just dropped the name of one of the world's leading fashion guides, Miles's face was completely devoid of any expression when Tressie's wide, unblinking eyes found his. She didn't realize that she had come to a sudden standstill in the grass until his arm moved from her shoulders to her waist and gently nudged her along. She stumbled forward clumsily, reeling from bomb he'd just dropped.

For the past fifty years, the *Manhattan Style Report* had been the be-all and end-all where fashion was concerned, and things were unlikely to change anytime soon. She had been a faithful subscriber for as long as she could remember, spending hours poring over the pages of the glossy magazine/newspaper hybrid and coveting most everything she saw there, including the prestigious byline credits. She shouldn't have been surprised that Miles had somehow acquired the legendary publication, but she was. Even more surprising was the opportunity that he was dangling in front of her face like a carrot.

"I see you're familiar with it."

"Yes, of course I'm familiar with it," she sputtered as she slowly climbed the steps to the rear veranda.

"Good," he chirped cheerfully, helping

Moira climb the steps, "because, in my humble opinion, it's really nothing more than a gossip rag. The only difference is, instead of following people and gossiping about *them,* you'd be following fashion and gossiping about *it.*"

"Oooh, that sounds like fun, doesn't it, Tressie?" Moira gushed as she eased down into a lounge chair. When she was settled, she handed off her cane to Miles and removed her floppy hat. Dropping it into her lap and shaking out her silver hair, she looked up at Tressie and smiled serenely. "You'd be able to travel all around the world while you're still young enough to enjoy it and do what you love without having to hide yourself from the whole world."

"Not quite the whole world," Tressie put in, sending Miles a pointed look. "Mr. Dixon here knew who I was without having to be told."

"It's my job to know who the major players in the industry are," Miles said easily. He pulled a chair away from the patio table with a flourish and motioned for Tressie to sit. No sooner had her butt hit the chair than he was leaning over her shoulder and whispering in her ear. "It's also my job," he said in a stage whisper, "to know when the time for change has come. Are you interested or not, Tressie?"

"Um . . ." Was she really ready to give up her plans for Vanessa Valentino? She wasn't completely sure. It was definitely something she'd have to take some time and think about. Vanessa Valentino had been her alter ego for over a decade now. Giving her up would be like parting ways with a dear friend. She needed to examine her thoughts and she how she felt about that. "Can I let you know?"

"Sure," Miles said, dropping into a chair at the table, stretching out his long legs and crossing his ankles. "Just don't take too long getting back to me. I'm only in town for the few days that it'll take me to help Moira get her plans for the annual fair off the ground, and then I'm returning to New York. When I get there, I'll be looking to fill that position immediately. Of course I'd like to have you on board, but if not . . ."

"Oh, Miles, stop badgering the girl," Moira butted in, swatting the air dismissively in Miles's direction. "She said she'll let you know and she will. So now that that's settled, let's move on to more important matters, shall we?" She beamed at Tressie. "Miles spoke to my attorney this morning, and you'll be happy to know that the initiative to have my estate designated as a historical landmark is moving right along. We should be hearing something any day now."

"Th-that's great, Moira!" It was an effort to sound appropriately excited, what with the possibility of an assignment with the *Manhattan Style Report* looming over her head and Miles literally breathing down her neck to either accept or deny it, but Tressie thought she did a decent job of pulling it off anyway. A historical landmark designation was exactly what the town needed, exactly what had to happen in order to save Mercy's way of life. If it happened, then she could go back to New York with a clean conscience, start a new life and never look back. "What about the situation with the town charter? What's going to happen with that?"

Moira's eyes sparkled. "First things first, my dear. We still have the fair to put on. After that, we'll see where we stand with the town charter situation. Something tells me, though, that everything is going to work out just fine. Now," she said, leaning forward and bracing her hands on her knees, "what date should we pick for the fair?"

The longer Tressie sat there, the more apparent it was that Moira wasn't going to settle for anything less than Tressie's complete involvement in pulling off what she was already proclaiming as the greatest town fair in Mercy's history. Tressie was surprised to learn that Moira had been practically consumed with the planning end of things, even though the dig was still under way on her property, and catering to the university's mounting publicity campaign had to be just as time-consuming. Between doing interviews for both the university's newspaper and the various media outlets that had begun to steadily trickle into town, conferencing with her attorney and navigating all the red tape that went along with historical landmark designation, Tressie didn't know where the woman found the time or the energy to worry about coordinating the town fair.

"What else do I have to do?" Moira asked when Tressie expressed her concern that Moira might be taking on too much. "Besides, I spoke to Pamela this morning, and she and Nathaniel are handling some of the arrangements on their end. Her tour is wrapping up in Long Beach tomorrow night, and then she and Nate will come home to help with things here. So don't worry, dear, we'll have plenty of help."

She was so excited, prattling on and on about the fair and how it would rejuvenate the townspeople, that she didn't notice the frozen smile on Tressie's face. Tressie had put it there a couple of minutes ago, as a sort of prelude to the little speech that she had prepared in her head, hoping that it would soften the blow when she told Moira that she planned to head back to New York long before the fair would take place. But now it served a totally different purpose — it kept her face from cracking into a million pieces and falling to the porch floor.

Nate was with Pam?

Suddenly everything made sense. It hadn't taken him a week to do the interviews that he'd scheduled. She had watched the interviews herself, had seen each one of them on television, and wondered after they were done when he would make his way back to Mercy and to her. She could've called him, she supposed, but she had wanted to see if he was thinking about her as much as she was thinking about him. So she'd waited for her phone to ring. And in a week's time, it hadn't.

Now she knew why.

As soon as he was done with his interviews, he had gone running off to be with Pamela Mayes. Tressie doubted that she'd even been a passing thought in his mind, not with the likes of Pamela Mayes to contend with.

Who was she kidding? This thing that she had going with Nate was and had always been just that — a thing. Never had that fact been more apparent to her than right now. If she hadn't known it before, she definitely knew it now, but that didn't stop her from wanting to throw something and scream at the top of her lungs. If she did either, though, Moira and Miles would think she was crazy, and under the circumstances, that was the last thing she wanted or needed.

Keep it together, Tressie, she told herself when she felt her plastic smile slipping sideways. *Keep it together for just a little while longer.*

It was definitely easier said than done, Tressie thought after two more hours had passed and a smile was still frozen on her face. The muscles around her mouth were screaming for relief, but if she didn't keep smiling, she knew she would probably break down and start crying like a baby. A couple of times, she caught Miles eyeing her curiously, as if he thought she might have a few screws loose, but she couldn't seem to relax long enough to calm her face and put on an air of normalcy.

By the time she'd managed to bid Moira

and Miles goodbye and make her way back to her hotel room, she was mentally exhausted but so out of sorts that sleep was out of the question. She hadn't absorbed much of anything Moira had said after hearing that Nate and Pam were together in California, and now it was all she could think about.

She took a shower and slipped into a nightgown on autopilot, thoughts of where Nate was, who he was with and what they were possibly doing swimming around in her head. When one too many images of Nate and Pam, naked and sweaty and wrapped around each other, flashed before her eyes, she squeezed them shut and burrowed underneath the covers to block them out.

She didn't realize that she had dozed off until her cell phone rang in the silence of the room and jolted her awake. She groped for it blindly, almost knocking over a lamp on the bedside table.

"Hello?"

"Tressie."

One word was all he had to say and her body was on full alert. Instantly wide-awake, she pushed back the covers and sat up on the side of the bed. "Nate?" She pushed her hair back from her face and cleared her throat. "Where are you?"

"I'm in California, sugar. Well, actually, we should be flying over California right about now."

We, he'd said. We. And then she heard herself saying, "We?" despite every cell in her body screaming for her not to. But she wanted to know, didn't she? More than that, she had to know. "You're with her, aren't you? That's where you've been all this time, isn't it? With her." She sounded accusatory, like a jealous shrew even to her own ears, but she couldn't help it.

"Tressie —"

"No, don't bother to explain, Nate. I understand perfectly."

The line was deathly quiet for several seconds, during which time Tressie wondered if he had hung up on her. A staticky announcement over the plane's intercom was the only indication she had that he was still there.

"Nate? Are you still there?"

"Yes, Tressie, I'm still here. Listen —"

Just then, a woman's sultry-sounding laughter wafted over the phone line and reached Tressie's ears. "Penny for your thoughts," the woman said, and Tressie gasped. Pamela Mayes sounded exactly the same, whether she was belting out a soulful ballad or making polite conversation.

"I have to go," Tressie blurted out.

"Tressie —"

"Goodbye, Nate."

"We'll talk when I get there, okay?" he said just as she took the phone from her ear and ended the call.

What was there to talk about? she wondered absently. If he was planning to let her down easy when he returned to Mercy and then parade around with Pamela Mayes right under her nose, then he could forget it. She couldn't stomach the thought of having to see him with another woman. She wouldn't stand it.

Miles, she remembered suddenly, had said that it was his job to know when the time for change had come. At the time, Tressie had only been thinking in terms of career paths, but now she was thinking about the broader picture. An affair with Nate Woodberry had been a bad idea to begin with. Miles had no way of knowing about her and Nate — at least, she didn't think he had any way of knowing — but his words were just now hitting home anyway. It was time for a change. She should've known it — should've seen it long before now.

Long before she found herself thinking about Nate at odd moments during the day and well into the night. And certainly long before she allowed herself to start imagining that there was something more than hot sex brewing between them.

But, as usual, she had jumped into a situation with both feet, without bothering to think about the consequences of her actions. For years, it was the way she'd worked, the way she'd operated. When she was hiding behind the facade that was Vanessa Valentino, reckless behavior was the fastest and most reliable route to getting the story she wanted. It was what had earned her a reputation in the industry and what had put her on top of her game. At this stage in her life, jumping in with both feet was pure instinct, and that instinct had never led her astray.

Until now.

Not once, but twice, Tressie thought bitterly, her propensity to leap before looking had come back to bite her in the butt. The backlash from her exposé on Gary Price and her subsequent and thinly veiled dismissal from the the *Inquisitor* because of it should've been her first clue. But *nooo,* apparently she hadn't learned her lesson, because, as soon as that part of her life had come crashing down around her, there was Nathaniel Woodberry. Recklessness in the flesh and beautifully masculine with it. Suddenly, ending a long period of celibacy had seemed like the best idea that she'd ever had, and in hindsight, it might actually have been so, if she'd just been able to keep her feelings out of the mix.

It had taken Moira's carelessly uttered words to show her that not only had she lost perspective since she'd come back to Mercy, but she'd also lost something much more important — her heart.

CHAPTER 9

Tressie lay in bed thinking until the sun rose the next morning. According to Moira, Nate wasn't due to return to Mercy until sometime tomorrow at the earliest. By then, if the Fates were with her, she'd be back in New York.

She'd whiled away the early-morning hours, thinking, plotting and planning, and now that the sun was shining and a new day had begun, she was thinking more clearly than she had since she'd arrived in town. As if she were channeling Vanessa Valentino, she climbed out of bed and crossed the room to an ancient rolltop desk. Returning to the bed, she sat down with a pen and a notepad, and scribbled down an impromptu to-do list for herself.

The house was empty, ready to go on the market as soon as the town's future was secured. She could afford to let it sit for the next little while, so she drew a line through that entry and moved on.

The project that she and Nate had collaborated on was done and was steadily making its way around the media circuit. Judging from the online feedback that the feature was receiving and the fact that the piece had almost instantly gone viral, she felt safe, if not a little nostalgic, drawing a line through that entry, as well.

Moira seemed to have the plans for the annual town fair under control, and the archaeological dig would probably be wrapping up soon. Thanks to Nate's influence, the university had pulled out all the stops where publicizing the find was concerned, and it, too, was beginning to garner national attention.

After drawing a line through that item, Tressie thought about the next item on the list, which was the town charter crisis. Truthfully, she wasn't sure if calling the situation a crisis was appropriate anymore. True enough, they hadn't received word on what the State of Georgia planned to do with the town. But it was a good sign that no in-town construction had begun and no representative from Consolidated Investments had been spotted around town, at least not since the Underground Railroad stop had been discovered.

Tressie liked to think that the powers that be were starting to see the light. She couldn't really pinpoint the whys and the hows, but she sensed that the situation would work itself out soon enough. Mercy was a strong small town, and Tressie couldn't see it just being wiped off the map. Its roots went deep and it would persevere whether she was here or not.

The line that she drew through that item was fainter than the others, but still visible. She would miss visiting with Moira.

Next on the list was one word. *Nate.*

In all the thinking that she'd done, she had skirted around one important issue. But in the light of day, it was easier to face it head-on than continue to avoid it. Leaving town before Nate returned with the only woman, besides his mother, that he had ever loved on his arm was essential. Hearing that he was with another woman had been hard enough. Seeing it with her own eyes would crush her. She'd always considered herself a pretty decent actress, and God knew that she'd had to act her way out of more than a few situations over the years, but this wasn't one that she was courageous enough to face.

It was bad enough that she had gone and fallen half in love with the least likely candidate to share her feelings. She'd be damned if she would let him know it. Nor would she ever again lose focus on what was really important.

Bidding Vanessa Valentino, her faithful alter ego for the past decade, a fond good-bye — at least for now — Tressie fished the business card that Miles had given her the day before out of her purse and picked up her cell phone from the nightstand. Miles was absolutely right, she thought again as she dialed the number on the card and listened to the phone ring on the other end. It was time for a change. She sucked in a deep breath and released it slowly, hoping that she was about to make a change for the better, because another bad decision was the last thing she needed.

"Dixon," Miles barked into the phone, breaking into her thoughts.

"Mr. Dixon, this is Tressie Valentine," she said before she could give in to the jittery nerves in her belly and change her mind. "I'm calling to accept your offer, with one small change in plans."

Miles chuckled smoothly, as if he had known that he would be hearing from Tressie again soon. "And that would be . . . ?"

"I have a few loose ends that I need to tie up, so I'm going back to New York tonight.

Can we pick things up there?"

"Penny for your thoughts."

Pam dropped into the seat next to him just as Tressie said, "I have to go." He heard the distress in Tressie's voice, but what could he do about it right now? Even if he was in a position to get into a heavy conversation with her, which he wasn't, Pam wasn't the type of woman to stand for being ignored for the time it would take to make his point. Whatever his point was. "Tressie —"

"Goodbye, Nate."

"We'll talk when I get there, okay?" She hung up, and he sighed long and hard. He let his eyes slide closed for a moment and then opened them back up on Pam's smiling face.

After spending nearly a week in her company, he was actually looking forward to the quiet of Mercy's days and nights. Before he'd left, he'd been feeling a little stifled, as if his creative juices were in danger of drying up if he didn't do something different quickly. Of course, being with Tressie had kept the feeling at bay for the most part, but still. There it was. But now that he had subjected himself to a grueling, nonstop concert schedule and more than a few all-night jam sessions, he could honestly say that his creative juices had nothing to do with the price of tea in China.

The problem, he thought as he switched on his Kindle e-reader device, slipped his glasses on and relaxed back in his seat as far as possible, was that he was getting old. While Pam had definitely been in her element, putting on impromptu performances and talking nonstop to just about every industry person that crossed her path, he'd spent most of his time ensconced in a corner of whatever room they happened to be in, nursing a drink and fending off the advances of scantily clad women who made it clear that they didn't often hear the word *no.* He hadn't exactly been bored, but he'd been damn close to it. The spontaneous getaway had been a nice little distraction, but he would've been lying if he'd said that he wasn't glad it was over.

By contrast, Pam was still on fire. Her twenty-city concert tour had sold out at every stop. On top of that, she was pumped up about an upcoming greatest-hits album and a *Recording Artists for Rwanda* CD that she and ten other artists were due to begin compiling in the fall. His surprise visit, she said, had topped off what had been a string of wonderful news, and she hadn't wasted any time showing him how happy she was to see him. He'd lost count of the number of times that she had hopped into his lap, burrowed into him for a hug and had to be gently but firmly ejected. Her behavior was nothing new and he'd never minded it before, but this time was different.

This time there was Tressie. . . .

"Penny for your thoughts," she said again quietly. Most of the other passengers in the first-class section of their flight were asleep. She had slept for most of the morning and well into the afternoon, so she was wide-awake and ready to talk his ears off.

"Right now they're not even worth that much," he admitted with a smile that didn't quite reach his eyes. "I was just thinking that it'll be nice to get back to Mercy. After keeping up with you for the past week, I'm in serious need of some R & R."

Pam's sparkling green eyes widened as she put a dainty hand to her chest as if to say, *Who, moi?* "You can't possibly be suggesting that it's my fault you're exhausted, Nate." A teasing glint lit her eyes and belied her offended tone. "If you recall, no one held a gun to your head."

No, he silently agreed, no one had held a gun to his head. He could've excused himself and gone back to his hotel suite at any time, but he hadn't wanted to leave Pam to her own devices for too long. There was nothing he could do when they were thousands of miles apart, which was most of the time, but he did what he could to save her from herself whenever they were together. He was well aware that she was a grown woman, but she'd been a walking time bomb for as long as he'd known her, which was forever. Good decision-making, especially when she'd been drinking, definitely wasn't one of her strong suits.

"You're right," he said, chuckling. "I should've known when enough was enough and conceded defeat. I guess I was under the mistaken impression that I could still keep up with you." He glanced at the lighted screen on his Kindle and secretly gave up on the possibility of getting any reading done. Besides the fact that Pam seemed determined to soak up every ounce of his attention, his mind wasn't on the latest *New York Times* bestseller.

Call her back, a little voice in his head suggested.

Later, he silently responded. Right now he needed time to think about what he would say when he did speak to Tressie again. She was upset — it didn't take a rocket scientist to figure that out — but he wasn't quite clear on why. And he never would be, he decided as he reclined his seat back and took off his glasses, if he didn't hurry up and figure out a way to silence Pam.

Hoping that she would eventually wind down, sort of like the Energizer Bunny, he slipped a sleep mask over his eyes and let his mind wander back to Mercy.

"What do you mean she's gone?" Nate asked for the third time.

Clearly exasperated, Moira pulled her robe tighter around herself and retied the belt at her waist. "For the third time, Nathaniel, Tressie left, going back to New York earlier this evening. I imagine she's there by now," she said, padding over to the stove in bright pink house slippers that matched her robe. "Now, would you like some warm milk or not?"

"No." Warm milk was the last thing, next to having his tongue cut out with blunt-tipped scissors, that he wanted. He had been poised to walk right back out the door after helping Pam drag a month's worth of luggage into Moira's foyer. Itching to be done with the farewells and small talk so he could make his way to Tressie, he had barely rolled the last bag to a stop when he'd asked Moira about her. And he had practically jumped down the woman's throat when she'd told him that Tressie was gone. Feeling bad for the way he had snapped at her, he took a breath for patience and tried again. "Listen, I apologize for biting your head off. I'm just . . . surprised. I didn't know she was leaving so soon."

"It was kind of sudden," Moira said as she walked back over to the table and poured steaming milk into two mugs. "I was hoping that she would help me finish plans for the town fair, so her leaving took me by surprise, too. But Miles is here and the three of you are helping me, so it all worked out." She took a seat at the table across from where Pam was sitting and patted the seat next to her. "Come and sit. Are you sure you don't want some warm milk?"

"Ah . . . no, no, thank you." His feet were already pointed in the direction of the rear veranda doors. "I, uh, should get home and get settled myself. I'll, uh, see you two in the morning." With a distracted wave, he was off. "P, I'll bring your rental back in the morning."

Unlike Pam, he had learned the art of packing light years ago. When he parked Pam's rental car in the driveway at his mother's house, the only thing requiring his attention was a rolling duffel and his carry-on. He grabbed those on the fly and took the porch steps two at a time, hoping that Moira had been mistaken and Tressie was somehow here. Inside, he dropped his luggage on the floor by the door and nudged it shut with his foot.

Well, I'll be damned, he thought as he pulled out his cell phone and pressed a button. No phone call, no note, no nothing. Just — bam! — gone. What the hell?

Nate glanced at his watch as the phone rang on the other end. It was half after two in the morning and Tressie had to be in bed, but the longer he held the phone and listened to it ring, the higher his blood pressure inched. Ring number one and he was curious. By ring number five, he was ready to go through the phone. At the end of the ninth ring, when the voice mail picked up and her cheery voice invited him to leave a brief message and a call-back number, he disconnected the call and cursed under his breath.

So it was like that? She had just breezed into town, talked her way into his work flow and into his bed, and then breezed right back out, without bothering to say goodbye? Who did that? And why? True, he and Tressie hadn't exactly discussed what it was that they were doing, but to his way of thinking, whatever it was, it was significant enough to warrant more than a disappearing act. If she hadn't wanted to continue seeing him, fine. If she was ready to move on, fine. No problem. But she could've at least given him the courtesy of saying something to him before she vanished. At the very least, a phone call would've been nice.

Almost as soon as the thought formed, Nate came up short and frowned at his own reasoning. His male ego was a little bruised, he could admit that, but he was a reasonable man — most of the time, anyway. He'd had many affairs over the years and they had all ended one way or another, some amicably, some less than amicably, depending on the personalities involved. This situation with Tressie was no different. It had to end sometime, and one of them would've had to end it. Pretty soon he would be packing up and heading back home to Seattle himself, so she had just beaten him to the inevitable.

That was what he was pissed about, Nate told himself as he stripped naked and stepped into the shower. She had beaten him to the punch.

That was all.

An hour later, as he finished setting up his

darkroom, switched on the red light and shut off the overhead light, he convinced himself that Tressie's leaving was for the best. She had simply saved him the trouble of having to break things off with her when the time came.

But, he thought snidely, she still could've called him.

He hadn't called.

Well, that wasn't entirely true. He had called once, the day after she'd left. But he hadn't bothered to leave a message and he hadn't called again since. And then she had called him back and the call had gone straight to voice mail, which meant that he was either out of service range or he had turned it off. She hadn't left a message.

And he hadn't tried to call again.

Now she knew why, Tressie thought as she stared at the computer screen in front of her. Images of Nate and Pam locked in one embrace after another were all over the internet. The one that showed Pam curled up in Nate's lap on an airplane was her personal favorite. They looked cozy . . . comfortable . . . as if they belonged together. The reporter in Tressie wondered how Pam's husband factored into the lovebirds' situation and how he felt about his wife and his supposed best friend's relationship. But the scorned woman in her couldn't have cared less about anyone's feelings but her own.

She was hurt.

She was disappointed.

She was —

The intercom on her desk buzzed. "Miss Valentine, the editorial meeting starts in five minutes, in the conference room."

Busy. She was busy. Too busy to waste time pining over a man who obviously hadn't wasted any time pining over her. She'd been back in New York for more than two weeks and he hadn't called, texted or emailed her once. She glanced at the slim gold watch on her wrist, then reached across her desk and pressed a button. "Thank you, Anita. I'm on my way."

As far as trade-offs went, she mused on her way down a long, plushly carpeted corridor lined with framed reprints of some of the magazine's most memorable spreads, a twentieth-floor office with a nice view of the Avenue of the Americas, an excellent six-figure salary and her very own assistant, all bundled into one neat, lucrative package, wasn't a bad deal. Not if the only other choice was a package filled with love triangles, emotional unavailability and great sex. A six-figure salary topped great sex any day, so she had definitely gotten the sweeter end of the deal.

In her head, that was a foregone conclusion. Now if only she could convince her heart . . .

To hell with her.

Every time Nate rolled over in the middle of the night, gritting his teeth and reaching for a painfully engorged and throbbing erection, that was the one and only thought that crossed his mind.

To hell with her.

Each and every time that he was at Moira's house and Moira mentioned anything that could even so much as loosely be affiliated with Tressie having been in Mercy, he wanted to say it out loud. But it never failed that Moira would start talking about the archaeological dig — about how nice the students had been, what an adventure the whole experience was and about how sad she'd been to see everyone go — and ruin the moment for him.

Every single time he heard the story, which had been something like fifteen times now, and she ended it by tossing in that silly little tidbit about how one of the maids finding a pair of pink-lace panties down by the creek had started it all, he went back to thinking it.

To hell with her.

Two weeks had passed and she'd only called him once. He'd missed the call and had quickly dialed into his voice mail, hoping that she'd left him something there, but she hadn't. So he hadn't bothered to call her back. He figured that whatever she'd wanted couldn't have been that important to begin with.

They didn't have a damn thing to say to each other at this point, especially since she obviously hadn't thought enough of him to at least share the news with him that she was now working for the *Manhattan Style Report.* Along with everything else, he'd had to hear that from Moira, too, which had really pissed him off.

So . . . to hell with her.

It wasn't as if he didn't have his own things to do. As much as he loved spending time with Pam and watching the precarious but friendly relationship between her and Moira develop, he knew that the time for him to part ways with Mercy, Georgia, had arrived. Julia, his publicist, was beside herself, worrying over the ridiculous notion that he'd had a mental breakdown in Mercy and was never going to leave. And that little voice in the back of his head, telling him that it was time for a new, more challenging and even riskier assignment, was getting louder and louder. For a while, Tressie had been enough of a distraction, but now that she wasn't a factor anymore, his adrenaline level was begging for a serious boost, the kind that fair planning couldn't even begin to provide.

He left the women to it and retreated to his darkroom to work on some of the projects that he had put on hold when the eminent domain crisis in Mercy had come up. There were rolls and rolls of film to sort through and catalog, and then he'd begin the arduous task of developing them. More than enough work to keep him occupied for at least the next week. That was how long Julia had said it would take her to finalize the arrangements for his next assignment, which he was hoping would take him to the edge of the earth and dare him to fall off. His instructions to Julia had been explicit. The riskier, the better.

He'd taken enough pictures of frolicking children and old men playing checkers to last a lifetime. It was time to get back in the trenches. Time, he thought as he switched off the red light and opened the darkroom door to the daylight pouring in, to finally get his mind right. Or to at least try. Holding up a still-dripping image of Tressie peeking out at him from behind a hundred-year-old oak tree, wearing a secret smile and absolutely nothing else, he wondered if that was even possible.

"You shot her."

Startled but not particularly surprised to find Pam curled up on his basement steps like a cat, Nate smiled absently at the picture she made. "I thought you and Moira were supposed to be working on the schedule of events for the fair?" he said.

"We were, but then Jasper showed up and all hell broke loose. When I snuck out, they were still arguing over whether or not to have the food catered. Jasper wants to barbecue, and Moira wants cold cuts and fruit spreads." Pam uncurled herself from the step she'd been wrapped around and got to her feet. She brushed off the seat of her denim shorts and slid past him into the depths of the darkroom. A corkboard hanging on the back wall caught her attention and she walked toward it slowly. "You shot her," she said again. Her tone was slightly accusatory, as if she suspected that he had committed some sort of crime but didn't quite know what the crime was.

She eyed the evidence at length, tipping

her head first in one direction and then another, checking out his work from different perspectives. In a few of the shots, Tressie stared back at her, smiling in some and looking either serious or distracted in others. In the majority of the shots, though, it was clear that she'd been unaware that her picture was being taken.

Nate knew the exact moment that Pam recognized the shots for what they were. Walking up behind her, he rested his chin on the top of her head and slid his arms around her waist. She leaned back into him and sighed. "You used to take pictures of me all the time," she said quietly. "I mean, like, *all* the time. You remember?"

"Every second of it, P." He dipped his head and gently pressed his lips to her hair. "Do you remember?"

"How could I forget? Those were some of the best times of my life. We were young and impulsive and —"

He found her hands with his own and threaded their fingers together. "Don't forget inconsiderate and selfish," he added.

"No one got hurt."

"True," he admitted aloud and sent up a silent thank-you. He had made his peace years ago with the fact that he and Pam had crossed a line in their relationship, hovered there together in a clandestine space for a time and then retraced their steps. Time and distance had allowed him to work through the guilt he had felt and put it behind him, but the photos that he had taken of Pam over the years were, and would always be, not-so-subtle reminders of the places they had been and the things they had done.

"It was good," Pam said.

"Damn good."

Nodding, she sucked in a deep breath and let it out slowly. "These are good shots. She's prettier than I remember."

Now it was his turn to nod. He couldn't think of a damn thing to say, so he didn't say anything.

"Damn, Nate. Either you're deliberately playing dumb with me or else you really have been in Mercy too long." She untangled her fingers from his and turned to look up at him curiously. "Why didn't you tell me you were in love with her?"

For the second time in as many minutes, Nate was at a loss for words. He stared down at Pam as if she had just spoken to him in a foreign language that he'd never heard before. Surely she was joking, he thought as he searched her eyes. She had to be. She stared right back at him, holding his gaze for long seconds and then finally shaking her head sadly. Having looked her fill, she proceeded to throw her head back and howl with laughter.

"You idiot," Pam blurted out when she could talk. She reached up and took his face in her hands. "You had no idea, did you?"

"I was starting to."

"So what are you going to do about it?"

"I don't know," he admitted quietly.

CHAPTER 10

A soft knock on Tressie's office door interrupted the silence. Distracted by the article draft that she was in the process of proofreading, she responded without bothering to look up. She figured that it was probably Anita, her assistant, bringing her the travel itinerary that she had been arranging for her review and approval. "Come in, Anita," she called out. On cue, the door opened and then closed. "You can just leave the itinerary in my in-box, and I'll take a look at it as soon as I'm done proofing this article."

Anita didn't respond, but then Tressie hadn't really been expecting a response. They were both new and still feeling each other out. Anita was fresh out of a Midwestern college, new to the city and almost painfully shy. Whenever she was required to speak, to Tressie or anyone else, she usually did so in brief spurts that consisted of one complete sentence or less at a time.

Tressie had been reading for at least five minutes before it occurred to her that she hadn't heard her office door open and close again. Sensing that she wasn't alone, she glanced up from the article spread out in front of her on the desktop and frowned. "Was there something else, Anita?"

Then she froze comically and stared.

"Anita wasn't at her desk," Pam explained as she dropped her purse into one of the chairs facing Tressie's desk and simultaneously sank down into the other one. "So I thought I'd take my chances and knock. I hope you don't mind."

"Um . . . of c-course not," Tressie practically sputtered.

In her line of work, she had rubbed elbows with more than a few celebrities, so she wasn't exactly starstruck at the sight of Pamela Mayes. She'd learned a long time ago that most celebrities were merely everyday people who had achieved celebrity status through a run of good luck or a tidal wave of tragic misfortune. At this point in her career, Pamela Mayes was a volatile mixture of both elements, but the fact that they had grown up together in the same small town made Tressie immune to the media hype. Her sudden speech impediment had nothing to do with being impressed and everything to do with the swift wave of jealousy that had come out of nowhere and punched her in the gut.

"What can I do for you?" Tressie heard herself say.

Pam's smile was one that she reserved for the paparazzi. "Actually, I was planning on asking you to do something for me. For old times' sake, I mean."

For old times' sake? Was she kidding? They had never been anything remotely close to friends growing up. Hell, they had never even been very friend*ly* toward one another. All these years later, Tressie couldn't think of anything that they could possibly have to discuss, let alone work together toward, if Pam's solicitous tone was any indication of where she was going with her bizarre request.

"I'm not sure I understand," she said slowly, carefully.

"Of course you don't. I'm not being very clear, am I?" A melodic laugh that Tressie was sure was meant to be self-deprecating floated out of Pam's mouth and hung in the air between them. A flicker of one delicate hand waved it away, and then Pam was back to being serious again. "I'm here because I need your help. Well, it's really more like Moira and I need your help."

At the mention of Moira's name, Tressie softened. Unfortunately, Pam's next words caused her to harden all over again.

"We'd like the *Manhattan Style Report* to be a part of the publicity campaign for this year's town fair, and we were hoping that, being from Mercy and all, you would take the assignment personally."

"The *Manhattan Style Report* is a fashion-industry publication," Tressie pointed out incredulously. "Our readers want to know what's going on in the world of fashion. I'm sorry, but Mercy is hardly the fashion capital of the world. I don't see what one has to do with the other."

"I didn't either until Miles pointed out the connection to me."

"Miles pointed out the connection to you," Tressie repeated flatly. It wasn't a question — more like a sarcastic missive. "How convenient."

"I know, right? While all of the other media outlets are reporting on the fair, you'll be there to cover the fashion aspect of it, with a little bit of a twist, of course. Miles told me that you're featuring an interview with Roberto Cavalli in next month's issue. So Miles and I thought, why not invite a few of my friends to perform at the fair and have them all wear Cavalli designs?"

"It's certainly an idea." And obviously Pam was nuts if she actually thought it was a good one. Gazing at her, Tressie wondered how the woman had gotten by all these years without someone picking up on the fact that she was clearly certifiable. Roberto Cavalli designs notwithstanding, the *Style Report* had about as much business at a town fair as a man-eating shark did. She was surprised that Miles was going along with such a ridiculous suggestion, if, in fact, Pam was telling the truth and he really was. With nothing but her body language to go on, it was difficult to pick up any clues as to whether or not she was stretching the truth.

It was easy enough to make a call and find out, though.

"I think I'd like to speak to Miles about this," Tressie said, reaching for her desk phone and sliding it closer to her. "Do you mind?"

"Not at all."

It took less than two minutes to get Miles on the phone, because Tressie had dialed his cell phone rather than his office line. While it rang on the other end, she sat back in her chair, crossed her legs and looked everywhere but at Pam. Though not as intensely as before, jealousy was still swimming around in her belly, and looking at the woman only made it worse. Pam could have any man she wanted, with her perfect hourglass shape, her slanted green eyes and her pouty, rose-tinted lips. And she imagined that all manner of men fantasized about having her. God knew she had been romantically linked to enough of them, despite the fact that she had an extremely good-looking husband waiting at home for her.

Why did she have to want the one man that Tressie couldn't have?

"Miles, this is Tressie," she said as soon as his voice came over the line. "I'm sorry to bother you, but Pamela is here in my office and —"

"Great, so she's already talked to you," Miles cut in, sounding relieved. "That's one less thing I have to remember to do today." Tressie heard papers shuffling in the background and then she recognized Janice's voice, asking him what he wanted for lunch. "Anything but liver and onions," he told her. Turning his attention back to Tressie, he said, "Listen, I know this is short notice, but with all hands on deck, we can pull it off. My assistant is handling the lion's share of the details, so there's nothing you need to do right now. You're leaving for Paris this evening, aren't you?"

She was covering a fashion show there over the weekend. "Yes, my flight leaves at six."

"Good. Have fun. We'll talk more when you get back."

She hung up the phone feeling that she had somehow just been hoodwinked and bamboozled, but the details of exactly how and when were a little fuzzy. Just about the only thing she was clear on was the fact that she was on her way back to the one place where she had absolutely no desire to return — Mercy, Georgia.

Pam waited until she was safely tucked into the back of the stretch limousine that was waiting for her at the curb before she pulled out her cell, pressed a button and put the phone to her ear.

"Is it done?" Nate said as soon as he picked up.

"Yes."

If Tressie thought that rubbing elbows with celebrities during her previous career had in any way prepared her for rubbing elbows with them in Mercy, Georgia, she was dead wrong. To any one of the five or six thousand people who had traveled to Mercy from parts both near and far to attend the fair, she was sure that the fair appeared to be moving along without a hitch. But to the select few, including herself, who were actually allowed to mill around behind the scenes, it was something else altogether.

Frankly, it was complete and utter chaos.

She couldn't help thinking that Vanessa Valentino would have had a field day with the myriad of hushed and not-so-hushed conversations that she managed to overhear in the process of doing the job that she was being paid to do. Emotions were running high, tempers were flaring and insecurities were rearing their ugly heads. It was a gossip columnist's idea of heaven on earth and a fashion reporter's worst nightmare.

Thankfully, Miles had agreed to let her bring along two of the magazine's interns as her assistants, because there was no way that she could be everywhere at once. And with two energetic and eager college students willing to do all the legwork, she didn't even try.

Armed with a notepad and a pen, in case she happened to have a need to take notes, and a micro-recorder, Tressie twisted and turned her way through the backstage crowds — which included a popular boy band that didn't look collectively old enough to be out past sundown, a chart-topping gospel duo who were about to take to the stage, and the ridiculously large entourage that surrounded a gold-laden rap star — and made her way back out front, where the spectators were. It was an outdoor lawn concert, and Truman Field was overrun with lawn chairs and blankets spread out in the grass. She chose the only out-of-the-way spot that she could find, a sliver of space off to the side of the stage, and sat down in the grass to watch some of the concert.

When Pam told her that she had called a few of her friends, Tressie had been thinking along the lines of one, maybe two performers. She hadn't been expecting the seemingly endless line of tour buses that had started rolling into town late last night. The last one, bringing the grand total to fifteen, had rolled into town just a few hours ago, and even Tressie had gasped in shock when the doors had hissed open and Mary J. Blige had appeared.

In the space of a few hours, Mercy, Georgia, had gone from being a tiny little nondescript town to being the site of a live benefit concert broadcast on several major cable-television channels. Just about everyone who was anyone was there, including the lieutenant governor of the State of Georgia. She knew because she had caught a glimpse of his motorcade cruising through town earlier in the day, heading toward Moira's estate.

The one person that she hadn't yet seen since she'd been back in town, though, was Nate.

Two hours later, the concert was still going strong, but Tressie's energy level was starting to fade. By the time the gospel duo was ready to perform a second song, she could barely keep her eyes open. Wanting to see what the chances were that she could head back to her hotel room, she sent text messages to her assistants, asking them to find her at their designated meeting place at the edge of the woods, and went there to wait for them.

Melissa appeared first and, anticipating Tressie, she had already organized her notes for Tressie's review. Jimmy was less organized but just as thorough. Tressie quickly scrolled through the digital shots that he had taken and gave them her seal of approval. Taking the notes and the digital camera and securing them in her tote bag, she gave them the rest of the night off. They headed back to the concert, and she had every intention of making a beeline for her room at the Mercy Motel.

Just as the thought of crawling into a soft bed and drifting off to sleep crossed her mind, an arm snaked around her waist from behind. She opened her mouth to scream — not that anyone was likely to hear her over the music — and was summarily cut off by the terse command in her ear.

"Shhh."

Instantly recognizing the voice, she whirled around to face Nate and immediately found herself being whisked into the thick of the pitch-black woods. "Nate? What are doing? Where in the world are you taking me? If you would just put me down, I could —"

In response to her query, he set her down on her feet and then backed her into a tree that was right behind her. Her head hit the bark with a soft thud, her mouth dropped open in surprise and then his tongue swept between her lips, stealing the last of her words.

Wider and wider, Nate forced her mouth open, until she was completely open to him and reveling in the sensation of his hungry mouth devouring hers. Every time his tongue stroked hers, she trembled at the corresponding sensations that snaked down her spine and settled between her thighs. She moaned into his mouth and swallowed his responding moan. Not trusting herself to touch him, she reached around behind her and gripped the tree trunk to steady herself as his hot onslaught continued.

Finally, Nate tore his mouth away from hers, but she only had a second to recover before his lips landed on the column of her neck and his tongue followed. He was creating a masterpiece of wet designs on her skin, as his fingers went to work on the knot of material tied at the base of her neck and dismantled her halter top. Her breasts came free and landed in the palms of his hands as if they had been specially created to fit there. He molded them, squeezed them, flicked the pads of his thumbs across them until she was panting and on the verge of begging him to suck them deep into his mouth and feed off them.

"Shhh," he hissed in her ear as the beginnings of a loud moan threatened to make its way up and out of her throat. "Shhh," he hissed again just before he dipped his head and granted her silent wish.

Sucking a nipple deep into his mouth, Nate trained his tongue on the tip of her succulent fruit and lapped at it lavishly. She couldn't have made another sound after that if her life depended on it. Her head fell back and her mouth stretched into a wide, delighted O as his rhythmic sucking motions perfectly mirrored the pulsing of her inner core. In time, he switched to her other breast and treated it to the same sensual attention. Then he pushed both her breasts together and slid his tongue from one marble-hard tip to the other until she was once again panting helplessly.

She was so disoriented that she didn't realize that he had slipped his hands underneath her dress until his mouth was inching along the crest of her breast and then gliding along the slope of her neck on its way back to her mouth. Only then did he allow her to feel his touch down below. His hands streaked across her thighs and teased the skin there, curled around her ass cheeks and squeezed.

"All the way over in Iraq," he growled in her ear, "I was thinking about this." One hand slipped inside her panties and claimed a cheek. "Us." The other hand followed suit. "You." As if to emphasize his point, his fingers homed in on their target just as he spoke the last word, sinking into her dripping-wet center from behind in a surprise assault that stole the last of her self control.

Tressie came hard. She came fast. And she came loud. Nate slanted his mouth over hers just in time to swallow her cries. After she had quieted, he withdrew his tongue from her mouth slowly and threaded his fingers through hers.

"Come with me," he whispered close to her face.

Holding tight to her hand, he led her deeper into the darkness of the woods until they came to a small clearing. He stopped walking and released her hand, leaving her to her own devices with only the quiet sound of his movements to guide her. "Nate?" She reached out blindly and breathed a sigh of relief when she felt his hand grip hers.

"I'm right here, sugar." A second later, he guided her hand down to where his penis was free in the night air. Needing no further encouragement, Tressie squeezed him gently and then began a rhythmic stroking that caused his heavy thickness to jerk in her hands. "Ah, yes, sugar," Nate groaned. "Damn, I missed you. Come here to me."

She had no idea what he was sitting on or how he had managed to find it in the darkness. But those were questions that would have to wait until later. Right now every fiber of her being was focused on following his nonverbal cues. Taking his hand once again, she closed the small distance between them and let him guide her down into his lap. Bracing her hands on his shoulders, she hovered in the air above him as he tugged her panties to one side and eased her down onto his straining erection.

"Oh, God," Tressie cried out. Then her eyes slid shut on a long, keening moan.

It was after two in the morning when they stumbled inside Nate's house, both of them out of breath and loose limbed with exhaustion. Unable to think straight because she was so sleepy, Tressie kicked off her shoes, dropped her tote bag at the foot of the bed and collapsed across the mattress. She was out like a light before her head landed on a pillow.

The thought of waking her and helping her get undressed crossed Nate's mind, but he quickly dismissed it. Deciding to let her sleep, he took a quick shower and retreated to the solitude of his darkroom to work off his exhaustion.

And to wait for Tressie to wake up so they could do what they should've done last night — talk.

He had watched her, stalked her, really,

throughout most of the concert, biding his time until he could get her alone so they could talk. Then when he was finally able to lure her away from the crowds and the noise, talking was the last thing on his mind. The last of his common sense had flown right out the window as soon as he had touched her. Pouncing on her like a wild animal hadn't exactly been his intention, but that was exactly what he had ended up doing anyway. Now that his common sense had returned, he was kicking himself for behaving like an ass.

What would he say to her when she woke up and came looking for him? What would they say to each other?

For the first time in his life, he was worried about what a woman thought of him — concerned about whether or not he could provide whatever she needed from him. He'd never really done relationships before, and the fact that he actually wanted to try his luck at being in one now scared the hell out of him.

Relationships meant commitment and fidelity and work and all kinds of other gray-area stuff that he'd never had the slightest interest in learning about. For all the reasons above, he had avoided committing to one woman like the plague, and now all he could think about was the one woman he wanted. His thoughts were so focused on her that, as exhausted as he was, he was nowhere near sleepy.

Developing film was busywork, something to do with his hands while his thoughts sorted themselves out. He moved from the sink to the counter and back again on autopilot, rinsing film, applying stop bath and following up with fixing fluid. Once it was safe to open the darkroom door, he hung the newly developed film on a drying line to drip-dry, and he set about cleaning up his mess.

Though he hadn't bothered to look up from his work in what must have been hours, he knew the exact moment that Tressie joined him in the basement. Oddly enough, he could sense her the way a wolf senses its mate. Without turning around to confirm her presence, he said, "Why did you leave?" He thought he knew, but he wanted to hear her say it.

"Because you didn't call when it mattered and then when you finally did, you were with her."

He did look up then, catching her eyes and holding them with his own. Even bundled up in his robe the way she was, he could smell the soap on her skin from her shower all the way across the room. Something inside him stirred and he wondered if she would push him away if he pounced again. "I wasn't sure what to say."

"I didn't think you wanted to say anything, especially after I saw the pictures of you and Pam that were plastered all over the internet. They were suggestive enough by themselves. Hearing her voice in the background when you called was . . ." She shook her head as if to clear it, looking a little lost. "Very hurtful," she finally said.

"Whatever those pictures suggested to you was incorrect."

He watched her push her fingers through her tousled hair and blow out a soft breath. "Listen, Nate, I know that you and Pam have a complicated past and, honestly, that's about all I care to know. You don't owe me any expl—"

"You came here," he cut in almost angrily. "You came here and you seduced me. And I let you, because I wanted you just as much as you wanted me. It was just sex." Her eyes widened in shock and she tried to look away from him, but he wouldn't let her. "In the beginning," he clarified slowly. "In the beginning it was just sex, Tressie. In the beginning. Do you understand what I'm saying to you?"

"I — I think so, yes."

He could see from the wounded expression on her face that she had absolutely no clue what he was saying to her. "I don't think you do, sugar. This is all new to me, so I'm not quite sure how to sweet-talk my meaning across to you. Forgive me if I don't put this to you the way one of those characters in a romance novel would, but I want to make sure I'm very clear."

Setting aside the cleaning rag in his hand, Nate crossed the room toward her deliberately. When they were standing face-to-face, he reached out and lifted her chin with his index finger and searched her eyes. "I'm not in love with Pam. How can I be when I'm in love with you?"

"Nate . . . I — I don't know what to say," Tressie whispered. A smile trembled around the edges of her lips, fighting a silent war with the tears swimming in her eyes.

"Say you don't mind that I don't have a ring for you right this minute," he suggested, his tone on the brink of pleading. "Say you don't mind that I haven't thought that far ahead just yet. Say you want to keep building on what we've started here in Mercy as much as I want to." A tear spilled over and rolled down her cheek slowly. He wiped it away with the pad of his thumb and flashed her a lopsided grin. "Better yet, Tressie, put me out of my misery and say you love me back."

A strangled cry broke free from her throat as she launched herself at him and wrapped her arms tightly around his neck. She burrowed into his embrace and unleashed a storm of tears. He might've had cause to be concerned about all the crying she was doing if she hadn't been laughing at the same time. "I told you all this was new to me, sugar," he said after several minutes had passed and she was still sobbing. "I'm going to need you to actually say something."

She reared back in his arms and gazed into his eyes. "I love you back, Nate Woodberry. There — is that what you wanted to hear?"

"Damn right," he said, laughing. As quick as lightning, he shifted her in his arms and helped her wrap her legs around his waist. Then he took the basement steps up to the kitchen two at a time.

"What are you doing?" Tressie shrieked.

"I'm taking you back to bed, sugar. I heard you say you love me and now I want you to show me."

EPILOGUE

Boom!

The deafening sound drew all eyes to the night sky just in time to see an explosion of bright colors fan out like a mystical umbrella overhead. Tressie blinked and then smiled, knowing that Jasper Holmes was somewhere behind the bandstand at the far end of Truman Field, having the time of his life. This was only the beginning, a dazzling introduction to what was scheduled to be at least an hour-long fireworks display. And from what she'd seen earlier of the stockpile of supplies that Jasper had amassed, it would definitely be a crowd-pleaser. Not wanting to miss a second of it, she dropped to her butt on the blanket that she'd spread out on the grass, then lay flat on her back so she could see nothing but sky.

The bright white sparkles that shot up into the sky every few seconds were almost as brilliant as the diamond solitaire on her finger, she thought giddily. Almost, because nothing in the world could outshine the ring that Nate had presented her with just three weeks ago.

She'd been completely unprepared for his proposal, such as it was. This past year that they had been together had been wonderful, but he hadn't so much as mentioned marriage and so she hadn't brought it up, either.

After last year's fair, they had left Mercy together and, aside from the time that they spent apart while each of them was on assignment, they'd been pretty much inseparable, dividing their time between his Seattle apartment and her New York loft. Their relationship had fallen into an easy rhythm that was both comforting and exciting, and if she had sometimes secretly longed for more, she was careful to pace herself. Nate wasn't the kind of man who could be cajoled or coaxed into doing anything, and she'd long since discovered that he was a true Southerner — slow as molasses about some things and lightning quick about others. Unfortunately, marriage seemed to fit into the first category.

Or so she'd thought.

Nate was in Dubai right now, finishing up a story and, she hoped, making his way back to her this very minute. He'd been away ever since the day he'd slipped the ring on her finger and then, while she was sleeping, quietly let himself out of his apartment in search of the nearest airport just before dawn. She had awakened to find the dazzling thing on her finger and a handwritten note, telling her that he loved her, lying on the pillow next to her. But not until she had connected with him via webcam, later that evening, did he speak the words to her and, by then, she was a nervous wreck.

Quickly, he'd said. He wanted to make her his wife quickly because neither of them was getting any younger and he wanted kids, two or three of them, at least. Did she want kids?

At that, she'd had to stop and really think about the question. Did she?

She hadn't really given it much thought until that very moment, hadn't really thought she would ever meet a man that she loved enough to make her think about having children. But Nate? Oh, yeah, she thought now as she listened to one explosion after another and marveled at the beautiful results overhead. She wanted every baby that she gave birth to to have his gorgeous hazel eyes and dimpled smile, his smooth chocolate-brown skin and his silky black hair.

Nate had smiled when she'd told him exactly that and said, "Quickly then, sugar. We'll do it quickly." As far as Tressie was concerned, he couldn't make her his wife quickly enough.

Apparently, Moira felt the same way, because she had offered the use of her estate for the ceremony and reception. Tressie hadn't seen the sense in arguing against being married on the south lawn, surrounded by Moira's legendary flower garden, especially since Moira had pointed out that the spot wasn't very far from the creek, where an as yet still-unclaimed pair of pink-lace panties had started it all.

Just thinking about that night made Tressie blush to the roots of her copper-streaked hair. By now just about everyone in town had figured out that the panties were hers, and she'd endured a variety of good-natured jokes about them. But then again, she had also been welcomed back to Mercy with open arms, so she supposed the trade-off was well worth it. After they were married, she and Nate would continue to divide their time together between New York and Seattle, at least for the next little while, but she couldn't imagine being married to the man she loved in any other place than the one they both knew as home.

As if to celebrate her thoughts, Jasper sent up into the sky a series of diving, sparkling things that shot off multicolored blasts of light. One after another, they exploded until Tressie was sure she had gone deaf from all the noise and blind from the brilliance of the light they gave off. She was so caught up in the loud and colorful presentation that at first she didn't hear her cell phone chiming. During a quick lull in the display, the sound finally registered and she dug the device out of her pocket hurriedly. The text message waiting for her stole her breath, made her heart beat at double time and curved her lips into a secret, feminine smile.

On my way to you, sugar, Nate had texted. I can't wait to make you mine.

It was late Friday night now, almost Saturday. They would be married in less than twenty-four hours.

Tressie couldn't wait, either.

The minute his plane touched down in Atlanta, Nate made a beeline for the exit and quickly claimed his bag from the conveyor belt. Rather than feel the slightest hint of trepidation about what he was about to do, he was literally on cloud nine. He'd been away from his woman for nearly a month now. And the closer he got to Mercy, the closer he got to the reality of feeling her soft touch and inhaling her sweet scent, the more he craved her.

He had come to the conclusion months ago that he was definitely, unequivocally and completely in love with Tressie Valentine.

The ring he'd given her had been his mother's, passed on to her by her mother, his grandmother, and, truthfully, when it had been passed along to him, he had never envisioned the day that he would slip it onto a woman's finger and make a solemn promise to her. He had thoroughly enjoyed his life as a bachelor and, now that he was thinking about it, he wouldn't have traded a day of it for anything in the world. Now he knew that it had prepared him for the here and now, and made him the man that he was today.

Was he scared? Hell, yes, he was. Who wouldn't be? Pledging your life to another person was risky in the best of situations, and God knew he had never been fortunate enough to witness a truly happy marriage firsthand. But he knew what he wanted, what he planned to build with Tressie by his side, what he was willing to work for, and living his life as a bachelor had succeeded in showing him that.

For the first time in maybe his entire life, he was completely and utterly happy. Globe-trotting and risking his life had filled a void in him that he hadn't realized was there until he'd found Tressie and then had to be away from her while he was on assignment. The stark contrast between the two extremes — foraging for information in hostile jungles on the other side of the world versus sharing his days and nights with Tressie — was glaringly clear. Once, he had believed that his work was all he needed in his life, but now he knew better. Tressie didn't yet know, but he had been laying the groundwork for scaling back on the overseas assignments that he accepted and setting in motion a plan that would allow him to be home with her as much as humanly possible. Not because he believed that marriage dictated that he should be, even though he believed that it did, but because he wanted to be. Work was work and he still loved it, but it wasn't enough. Not anymore.

As usual, Julia had arranged for transportation to be waiting for him at the curb outside the airport. After tipping the valet, he tossed his bag into the trunk and then slid into the front seat of a sleek Chrysler SUV. It was a little slicker than he usually preferred, he thought as he eyed the spaceship-style console, with all its buttons and knobs and bells and whistles, but it would do. He pressed a button to kick-start the air-conditioning, found an all-news station on the satellite radio and tapped the in-dash computer screen to shut off the voice-activated navigation system. Before driving away from the curb, he pulled out his cell phone, set it up to recharge the waning battery and shot off a text to Tressie.

On my way to you, sugar. I can't wait to make you mine.

In less than twenty-four hours, she would be. A smile curved his lips as he reminded himself that he owed Pam an as yet unspecified amount of cash. Every time the topic of whether he would ever get married came up, the amount at stake always increased by leaps and bounds. Of course, he'd always been for the con and Pam for the pro, and bets had been made. One day, she'd sworn, a woman was going to come out of nowhere and knock him flat on his ass. He'd always laughed at her, but, as it turned out, the joke was on him. Once or twice over the years, he had entertained the idea that maybe that woman was Pam, but fate and common sense had disabused him of that silly notion years ago. Pam had never really knocked him on his ass, not the way Tressie had, and now that he was thinking about it, he came to the conclusion that Pam had figured that out long before he finally did.

He was idling in the long line of cars waiting to exit the airport's parking complex when his cell phone vibrated in the passenger seat. He had an incoming text message.

Tomorrow.

The simple, one-word reply from Tressie wrapped a fist around his heart and squeezed.

Yes, tomorrow, he texted back just before he set aside the phone and turned his attention to the drive ahead of him.

It was a simple ceremony, with just a handful of close friends in attendance, a beautifully tended flower garden as the backdrop, and the minister who had baptized both Nate and Tressie ages ago officiating. Neither of them had wanted anything lavish. Aside from joining hands to light a candle for his mother and for her grandmother, nothing about the day's events was traditional.

Moira had argued for a customary wedding dress, but Tressie's heart was set on an ivory linen shift that she'd found among

Ma'Dear's things when she was packing up the house. She had instantly recognized it, having seen it every time her gaze landed on the photo of her mother that was on the mantel in her apartment, and claimed it for her own. The idea to be married in it hadn't come until after Nate had proposed to her and the reality of not having any real family there with her on her special day had fully set in. This way, she'd told Moira just that morning, a little piece of Geneva Valentine would be there in spirit.

Now, as she made her way down the grand staircase in the main house and paused in the foyer to take one last look at herself in the ornately framed mirror there, she knew that she had made the right decision. The dress fit her perfectly, with its fitted strapless bodice and flowing calf-length skirt. It was as if it had been just waiting for her to stumble upon it and realize what it was there for.

And maybe it had been, Tressie conceded as her gaze fell upon the delicate strand of ivory-colored pearls around her neck. They were Ma'Dear's, and her grandmother had worn them to church every Sunday as far back as Tressie could remember. Same with the matching pearl studs, she recalled, and delicately touched a finger to one of the posts in her ears. Wearing them today was the next best thing to having Ma'Dear there with her.

"Stop fussing," a voice said from behind her. "You look great and I should know, because I did your makeup myself."

Tressie spun around to face a smiling Pamela Mayes. "Thank you again for that. I couldn't seem to make my hands stop shaking." She held them up in front up her and looked at them. "They're still shaking."

"Believe me, Nate's are, too, so you're in good company. Here, I believe this is for you." Pam produced a single red rose with a flourish and handed it to Tressie. "Do you need anything else before I go outside?"

Tressie returned Pam's smile and shook her head, no. They weren't quite friends but she thought that maybe someday they might get there. "No, I think I'm as ready as I'll ever be."

"All right, then, I'll go let everyone know that we're ready to begin." Reaching for her hand and squeezing it, Pam turned toward the row of French doors leading out to the back veranda. Tressie watched her through the glass as she descended the steps gingerly in four-inch heels and tipped across the manicured lawn to stand beside her husband in the small crowd gathered on the garden's brick center island.

Seconds later, a lone violinist began playing a winsome, haunting melody, and Tressie alighted from the main house. On some level, she registered the fact that all eyes were on her as she descended the steps, but she only had eyes for Nate. Months and months ago, she had compared him to a warrior, and the comparison still was true today. A soft breeze played with the silky hair lying on his wide shoulders and rustled the loose-fitting ivory linen suit he wore. He should've looked romantic and sensitive, but instead, he was somehow even more fierce-looking. She held his eyes and watched him watch her as she approached and joined him underneath a cedarwood arbor, wondering what he was thinking.

Fortunately, she didn't have to wait long to find out. They joined hands to light candles for their loved ones and then turned to the solemn minister.

"I can't help thinking," the minister began, his gravelly voice reaching out and touching the small crowd, demanding that they pay attention, "that something about the Southern skies makes romance a little more exciting and love a little sweeter."

Nate caught Tressie's eye and winked.

"Nothing pleases the universe more than

when two souls come together as one," he continued. "And nothing pleases me more than witnessing two souls that I've known ever since they were babies come together as one. Before we begin, Nathaniel and Tressie have prepared their own vows." He motioned to Nate. "Nathaniel?"

Tressie was startled to see tears swimming in Nate's eyes when they faced each other again. As soon as he blinked and a tear rolled down his cheek, she released his hand just long enough to reach up and swipe it away. He caught it before she could thread her fingers through his again and pressed a kiss to her palm.

"Tressie," he said, then released a shuddering breath. "I'm not perfect, but I'm convinced that everything I've ever done in my life, every decision I've ever made, has been so that I would be prepared to meet you here today and give you my heart. I love you, sugar. Everything I am, everything I have and everything I can be, I give to you, forever and always. I'm only going to do this once and you're it, sugar."

He fell silent, staring down at her, waiting. It was her turn. She was supposed to say something, supposed to recite the vows that she had been practicing ever since she was twelve years old, but the words wouldn't come. She couldn't squeeze them out around the lump in her throat. He squeezed her hand gently, encouraging her to speak, but she just couldn't. His words had stilled her, stolen her voice and quieted her mind. For the first time in her entire life, she felt complete . . . and safe . . . and at peace. Nothing she could say could ever communicate what she was feeling to him. It was too big and she was too full with it to even make sense of it herself.

He seemed to sense what she couldn't say, though, if the slow, lopsided grin that took over his mouth was any indication. Seemed to understand that she was full right now and needing a moment to gather her scattered thoughts and somehow string them together. She swallowed once, then again, and opened her mouth. Tears came then and they had to be dealt with. Moira produced a crumpled tissue and Pam stage-whispered something to her about not ruining her mascara even as she took the tissue that Moira offered, dabbed at her eyes and probably did just that.

When she was reasonably sure that she had her emotions under control again, she passed the tissue back to Moira and reached for Nate's hand again. Clearing her throat, she opened her mouth and tried again. This time, she managed to find her voice. "Nate . . ."

Silence.

"Yes, sugar?"

"Oh, to heck with this. . . ."

Tressie launched herself at him and wrapped her arms around his neck, holding on for dear life. His arms instinctively caught her, but his mouth went slack with surprise, which was just fine with her. His lips were in the perfect position for her to dive in and let her lips speak to his . . . from the heart.

ABOUT THE AUTHOR

Terra Little has been reading romance novels for decades and falling in and out of love with the heroes within the book covers for just as long. When she's not in the classroom teaching English Literature, you can most likely find her tucked away somewhere with her laptop, a dog-eared romance novel and romance so heavy on the brain that it somehow manages to weave its way into each and every story that she writes, regardless of the genre.

Terra resides in Missouri, but you can always find her on the World Wide Web to share feedback, the occasional joke and suggestions for good reading at writeterralittle @yahoo.com. Visit her official website at www.terralittle.com.